REFUGE

WILLIAM KINREAD

Fisher King Publishing

REFUGE

Published by
Fisher King Publishing
www.fisherkingpublishing.co.uk

Copyright © William Kinread 2024

Trade Paperback ISBN: 978-1-916776-33-3

Ebook ISBN: 978-1-916776-34-0

All rights reserved. No part of this publication may be reproduced or distributed in any form or by any means, or stored in a database or electronic retrieval system without the prior written permission of Fisher King Publishing Ltd. Thank you for respecting the author of this work.

This is a work of fiction. Names, characters, businesses, places, events and incidents are either the products of the author's imagination or used in a fictitious manner. Any resemblance to actual persons, living or dead, or actual events, is purely coincidental.

Printed and bound by CPI Group (UK) Ltd, Croydon, CR0 4YY

To the real Dr Ben Mercer

Prologue

A refuge is a place of safety. Safety from danger. Safety from extreme weather. Safety from those of whom we are afraid. But it can also become a prison. A place we are too scared to leave.

The Psalmist says we should walk through the Valley of the Shadow of Death, not sit down and dwell in it. A refuge should, therefore, provide a temporary respite. It should be a sanctuary in which to recover before the fight back begins.

Chapter One

Winter 1999

It was the second week into the New Year and the traffic in Harrogate was getting back to normal as people returned to work and children to school after the festive break.

Ian parked his E-type Jaguar on Beech Grove, let Sky off the rear bench seat and started walking across The Stray towards his office. The rains of November and December had been replaced by a drop in temperatures and the ground was hard with frost. The sky was a thick grey and a freezing fog made it feel even colder than the gauge would suggest.

It made a gloomy start for a Monday morning. Ian felt the rawness bite through his clothing and thought it was going to snow. He turned up the collar of his Crombie overcoat and thrust his hands into the pockets.

It had not actually started out as his overcoat. It was his father's and, consequently, the length was too short, the sleeves revealed too much cuff and it was too big in the body.

Anderson & Sheppard, the Savile Row tailor, had

done what it could, but a bespoke coat that was made for someone five feet ten inches tall and weighing 14-and-a-half stone could not easily be converted for someone six foot two and weighing two stone less.

It was also old. About 50 years old to be precise but, nevertheless, Ian liked it. He had worn it at his father's funeral when, as a 16-year-old boy, it had almost swamped him. After the Anderson & Sheppard alterations, he wore it at university with jeans, which looked quite fashionable, and in his first flat, with its single-glazed windows, where he put it on his bed and used it as a blanket. Now its charcoal- grey colour suited the formal attire of a solicitor and the 35-ounce cloth protected him against the rigours of winter.

Ian even considered it looked quite chic as he entered the office with a sprinkling of snow, or frost that brushed off the trees, scattered about his shoulders.

When Holly said: 'You really will have to buy yourself a new coat,' he was, therefore, somewhat surprised. It was not the reaction he had been expecting.

Holly was Ian's new secretary, Debbie, his previous one, having moved to Spain. She was highly attractive with mid-length, warm-brown hair, and grey/green eyes, but she was married and, in fairness to Ian, he didn't think of her in that way. It was her common sense and personality which had convinced him that she was ideal for the role of what really amounted to his personal assistant.

'Why, what's wrong with it?' Ian asked indignantly.

'Well, it doesn't fit you,' Ed replied, laughing from his desk in the corner.

'And it's threadbare,' Holly responded.

Ian lifted his left arm in the way you would if you looked at your watch and inspected the sleeve. There were a few shiny patches where the wool had worn smooth and there was some fraying around the pockets.

'Well, it keeps me warm, so it will just have to do for now,' Ian said, and then, clapping his hands together once, he continued: 'So, what's on the agenda for today?'

'I've had a telephone call from someone called Graham Towers,' Holly said, but before she could finish, a woman burst into reception. She looked about 60 and seemed a little flustered. She moved her head from side to side, looking at Holly and Ian, wondering to whom she should address her question and then, just blurted it out so that they both could hear.

'If I bring my neighbour in, can you do a will for him?'

'Of course,' Ian replied.

'He's 93.'

'Is he compos mentis?'

'Oh, yes. He's as bright as a button, but he can't drive. I live next door and keep a motherly eye on him.'

'Well, there shouldn't be a problem. I will have to see him on his own, though, but you can wait in reception if you wish and have a coffee with Sky,' Ian said, looking towards the dog. Sky had a very useful calming effect on clients to such an extent that Ian joked he would have to put her on the payroll.

'Can I bring him in this afternoon?' she asked anxiously.

Ian looked enquiringly at Holly and she nodded.

'Yes, that should be fine. Is 2pm okay?' he asked.

'Yes. Thank you.'

'And your name is?'

'Penny Carr.'

'And your neighbour is called?'

'Roly Pound.'

'Very good, Mrs Carr?' Ian said, emphasizing the Mrs in a questioning sort of way.

She nodded and replied: 'I'm a widow.'

Ian shook her hand. 'I will see you both later.'

Once she had left the office, Ian turned to Holly and said: 'That's funny.'

'What?'

'Well, she's called Carr and she's the driver!'

'Ha-ha! Now can we get back to Graham Towers please?'

'By all means,' Ian replied, smiling mischievously.

'He lives in the middle of nowhere on the North Yorkshire Moors, somewhere near Helmsley. Apparently, he bought a house with 30 acres and the local hunt have been crossing his land without his permission. He wants you to stop them and he wants a home visit.'

'Mmm, I'm not sure if that's our sort of thing. More litigation, really.'

'He said he didn't care what it cost.'

Ian raised his eyebrows. 'That's interesting. Might be worth a look. I suppose we could go on the grounds of trespass rather than getting bogged down in the rights and wrongs of fox hunting. Can you call him back and make an appointment for me to see him tomorrow afternoon, please?'

'Yes, boss,' Holly replied with a friendly familiarity that had quickly developed between them.

Ian immediately liked Roly Pound when he wandered into reception. Penny Carr, having opened the door to the office, stuck her head in and said she would come back after doing some shopping.

He was slightly built but looked fit and lean, and he was smartly dressed in a dark-green tweed suit, flecked with specks of tan and lighter green. It was the sort of suit that was made for a labourer in a bygone era out of a hardwearing cloth, with deep pockets and baggy trousers. He also had a sparkle in his eyes.

'Hello, Mr Pound, come on in. Would you like a coffee or a tea perhaps?'

'A cup of tea would do nicely,' he replied.

Ian looked at Holly and, as she headed for the kitchen,

Ian led Mr Pound towards the meeting room. Sky got up from her basket in the corner by Ian's desk and followed.

'You don't mind if Sky joins us, do you?' Ian asked. 'She will keep everything confidential.'

Mr Pound smiled at her. 'I don't mind at all. Collie, is she?' he asked, prompted by her tricolours of black, white and tan, although he was puzzled by the long nose.

'Yes, she's a Smooth Collie. Like Lassie but with a short coat,' Ian explained, as Mr Pound gave an exaggerated nod to indicate his enlightenment.

The ground floor of the office had two large rooms to the front. One comprised a well-appointed reception and the other was Ian's office, which he shared with Ed. The two rooms were divided by a beautiful, bespoke light-oak set of cupboards, which had a frame from waist height to the ceiling, encompassing two large glass panels in between. It was designed to enable everyone to see what was going on, as they would not all be in the office at the same time.

The rooms to the rear comprised a kitchen, cloakroom and comfortable meeting room with a circular glass coffee table and leather armchairs. Every room had a fireplace, but in the meeting room it was particularly large and made quite a feature. Upstairs was a two-bedroom flat which Ian let out.

'So how can I help you?' Ian asked.

'I would like a will and I want to leave most of my

money to someone I've never met,' Mr Pound said playfully.

Ian smiled kindly. 'Would you like to elaborate?' he asked.

'I thought I would die first, but my wife died before me. If she had survived me, she was going to leave everything to her best friend, Margo, but she's in her eighties now so I thought I would leave it to her son.'

'Do you know his name? And address?'

'He's called Philip Jennings. I don't know his address, but I can give you Margo's and you can get it from her after I'm gone.'

'So I'm assuming you and your wife didn't have any children?'

'No!' Mr Pound replied, laughing out loud. 'We only got married when I was 65. I worked for the National Trust as a gardener until I retired and I lived in a tied cottage. When we got married, I moved into my wife's house, you see, so I consider most of the estate belongs to her and I want to honour her wishes.'

'Makes sense,' Ian acknowledged. 'You said you wanted to leave most of the estate to Philip Jennings. Is there someone else you want to benefit as well?'

'Well, I'd better leave Penny something - £5,000 I'd say, although she will be expecting more.'

Ian smiled. 'She did seem quite anxious to get you here,' he said light-heartedly.

'Yes, well she looks out for me, but £5,000 is enough. And I want to leave £10,000 to the village cricket club and £10,000 to the village hall fund.'

Ian was taking notes and looked up.

'Anything else?'

'No, the rest is to go to Philip.'

'Do you know how much your house is worth?' Ian asked.

'Well, they reckon £150,000, but they haven't seen inside it! Crazy, house prices! The young can't afford to get married nowadays.'

'Who's they?'

'The estate agents. I thought you would ask me, so I rang up for a rough valuation.'

Ian bowed his head slightly to the side and raised an eyebrow indicating approval.

'Any cash or other assets?'

'£50,000 in the building society. Nothing else.'

'Final question. Have you given any thought to executors?'

'I'd like you to do it because I haven't got anyone else.'

'That's fine, but you need two really, so I will add my colleague Edward Tucker if that is all right with you?'

'If that's what you recommend,' Mr Pound replied.

'I do,' Ian said just as he heard the front door open. Penny Carr was back.

'Well, thank you for coming in, Mr Pound. I think I've

got enough to go on for now. If you can telephone me with that address, I will prepare a draft will for you to look at and then we can take it from there.' Ian stood up and offered Mr Pound a helping hand, thinking the soft leather armchairs might prove a challenge, but Mr Pound didn't need any help. He was remarkably fit for his age. He straightened himself up and shook Ian's hand.

'Roly,' he said. 'Call me Roly.'

The next day was brighter. The fog had cleared and a bright blue sky lifted everyone's spirits, even though there was still a brisk breeze to chill the blood.

The drive to Thirsk was mundane, but, once Ian turned off the A170, the beauty of the North Yorkshire Moors National Park became apparent. He drove through Kilburn, the home of Mouseman oak furniture and the White Horse, and on to the pretty village of Coxwold, where the cottages of former agricultural workers now cost a fortune. He then drove past Ampleforth College and reminisced to himself about an 800m race he had competed in when he was a pupil at Sedbergh School and, finally, as he came into Oswaldkirk, he took the road north to Helmsley and turned off after a couple of miles to the home of Graham Towers.

The property had been carved out of a landed estate and sold off during hard times, so Ian drove up the straight tarmac drive towards the stately home and then took a

90-degree turn to the left at a sign marked 'Middle Wood Farm.'

The narrow tarmac road continued until Ian reached some wooden gates which opened automatically and then the tarmac-surfaced area broadened considerably. In front of him was a roundabout formed by a low dry-stone wall with a tree planted in its centre and behind that was a huge garage with a gable end facing the front. The large oak doors of the garage were open and Ian could see a blue BMW 7-Series and a silver Mitsubishi Shogun parked inside, along with a gypsy caravan in the left-hand corner and numerous bits of smaller machinery, such as lawn mowers, filling the remaining space. The house, which was a barn conversion, was offset to the left of the garage and, whilst attractive, it was somewhat cramped and overshadowed by the garage, which was obviously newly built.

To the right of the garage was a wood. Perhaps that was 'Middle Wood,' Ian thought. To the back of the house and around the sides were large expanses of open land which looked arable in nature.

Ian knocked on the front door and a woman with short grey hair, styled like a man's and of medium build, opened it.

'Hello, I'm Ian Sutherland. I've come to see Mr Towers.'

'Oh, yes. I'm his wife, Kath. Come in.'

Mrs Towers led Ian into the kitchen, which was large, long and had every modern facility. There were lots of marble surfaces, light oak cupboards and stainless-steel equipment, but no Aga.

A border collie bitch cowered in the corner and Ian bent down to stroke it, but it shot down the hallway and vanished out of site just as Graham Towers walked into the kitchen.

'You won't get a hand on her - she was mistreated,' he said.

'Oh, no, what happened?' Ian asked, foregoing any introduction which Mr Towers obviously thought unnecessary.

'I don't know. Reckon she's been brayed. We haven't had her long. Got her from the RSPCA in York,' he said gruffly.

Ian shook his head. 'I can't bear cruelty to animals. I think the perpetrators ought to receive the same treatment.'

Graham smiled and shook Ian's hand. It was the rough handshake of a labourer. Ian's hand felt slightly crushed and he stretched it when freed.

'Drink?' Mrs Towers asked.

'Erm,' Ian hesitated.

'We haven't time for that,' Graham replied quickly. 'I want to show him round back.'

Graham led the way down the hall into a sitting room and conservatory, and then through some double doors to the back lawn. A large, kidney-shaped swimming pool took centre stage, beyond which was a big, square field. Mrs Towers had followed behind them.

Graham turned around and pointed to the driveway.

'Kath had just come out to hang up some washing when the hounds came down our drive, over the garden fence and then into our field. Some stopped to drink out of our pool and one got caught by its back leg on the barbed wire. She was trying to free it when the horses came down the drive and the Master asked for permission to cross our land. She said: "No, my husband wouldn't like it," and he said: "You ought to be bloody grateful, woman. That fox killed four geese last night."' Graham's voice was rising and he started pointing, not at Ian, but by way of emphasis.

'It's lucky I wasn't here,' he continued, 'because, if I had been, I'd have shot him.'

People says these things without meaning them, but in this case Ian wasn't so sure. Graham looked as though he was serious.

'Do you know what the Master is called?' Ian asked.

'Major Urquhart.'

'Well, I could write to Major Urquhart in his capacity as Master of the Hunt and we could reiterate that access to your land is refused and point out that any further infringement will be treated as trespass. Then, if they do it again, we could apply to the court for an Injunction and damages, although any damages will probably be minimal.'

Graham walked over to a wrought-iron table and chairs which were painted white and sat down awkwardly. His right hip seemed to be giving him some pain. He pulled a large cheque book out of his back pocket and slapped it on the table.

'Have you got a Biro?'

Ian handed one over.

'When we got married, I had a ten-shilling note in my back pocket.' Mrs Towers nodded by way of affirmation. 'Now, we can buy anything we want, but we've no children.' For a moment he stared at the ground.

'Foxes come from that wood there.' He pointed to the wood behind him. 'I feed them on an evening. And badgers. And we've got deer, owls, all sorts.' He paused whilst he signed a cheque. None of the other details were filled in. He ripped the cheque out of the cheque book and handed it to Ian.

'I don't care what it costs. I never want to see them on my land again and tell that Master, if I do, I'll shoot him.'

'Well, hopefully that won't be necessary,' Ian said jokingly. 'But there's no need to give me a cheque. You can pay me later.'

'No. Take it. You'll see I'm a man of my word.'

'Well, I will let you know before I fill it in. I'll write a letter to Major Urquhart and see how he responds, and then I will be in touch.'

'Very good,' Graham said, as he twisted awkwardly on the chair and pointed to a garden gate. 'Kath will show you to your car.'

The simmering sun had warmed the air, the wind had dropped, and as Ian headed home, the western horizon was streaked with orange.

He started thinking about foxes and his mind wandered back to John Field, his seminal client, who had been a sniper in the Second World War. The man who had shot SS-Hauptsturmfuhrer Manfred Fuchs. A shudder ran down his spine as he remembered how Fuchs's son, Frederick Granville, had tried to kill him. And he thought about Sophie, his now ex-girlfriend, sitting in Bettys when she saw his chocolate brownie with the face of a fox and pointed out that Fuchs was German for fox.

He shook his head and tried to think of something more positive, but maybe it was telepathy because Frederick Granville was sat in northern Cyprus thinking about Ian.

It was raining and cold as Granville looked out over the Karpass Peninsula, swirling his Raki in his glass so that the ice turned it cloudy. 'Lion's milk' they called it. He sipped up some of the aniseed spirit and started to channel the thoughts of a predator.

He had been sentenced to 10 years in prison and served five. His grandfather, Lord Granville, had died. They had lost Florin Hall, the family estate, and his mother was now a grace-and-favour tenant in her former home, a converted stable. Oh, the ignominy of that! They had even lost the bank or, rather, the English bank. He still had the Zurich branch, which had been a separately registered Swiss subsidiary, but, as its parent company had gone, it was like a lifeboat bereft of its mother ship.

He had tried to emigrate to Switzerland, but residency was refused owing to his criminal record. So now he found himself in northern Cyprus, where there was no extradition treaty, which he thought might be a useful safeguard as he tried to rebuild his fortune. He hoped this would be created by his new bank in Nicosia, which was specialising in money laundering for the recipients of the incredible wealth haemorrhaging out of the former Soviet bloc following the fall of the Berlin Wall.

He was keen to recreate his fortune. To escape from this open prison. To put his family back on the map. But there was one emotion that burned much more strongly. One emotion that consumed him. One emotion that occupied every breathing minute. That emotion was revenge.

Chapter Two

Funnily enough, Frederick Granville was not the only person desirous for revenge, but whilst Granville's hate was directed towards Ian, Simon Black's detest was centred on Granville.

Of course, Black's appetite had been partially satiated by the death of Lord Granville and the demise of the Granville empire, but a kernel of loathing remained for the scion of his nemesis. The last thing he wanted was for the old banking empire to rise from the ashes. Only total destruction would suffice.

However, such thoughts were far from his mind as he lay on his lumpy bed at The Grand Hotel in Pristina, reading the latest press releases from Sky News. Unsurprisingly, they were more up to date than MI6.

His telephone rang and a hotel receptionist said a guest was waiting for him in the hotel bar. Black leapt to his feet, keen to leave the depressing surroundings of his bedroom. He didn't usually leap anywhere but he must have moved suddenly because a flock of pigeons took off from the upper floors and circled over the smouldering buildings below.

Black walked over to the window and closed it. In fact, Foreign Office advice was to keep it closed at all times, along with the curtains, but he couldn't stand the smell of damp and mould. He saw a family trudging down the road, pulling a hand-drawn cart containing their worldly belongings and he thought back to his own flight from the Red Army all those years ago. He didn't feel particularly sorry for the family. He knew what it was like to be cold and hungry and in fear of one's life, nevertheless, he closed the curtains to block out the memory. It wasn't the hardship that bothered him. It was the fact that Lord Granville had separated him from his family without giving it a second thought.

Dragging himself from this reverie, he navigated a maze of dimly lit corridors, their moss green carpets and mushroom brown wallpaper matching perfectly the grey concrete structure of the building, until he reached the lobby. There was no way he would risk the lift. If it broke down, which was likely, he might never be rescued.

The hotel lobby with its dark grey marble floors and moss green, square-sided, leather chairs, stank of cigarette smoke but, at least, it only stank. The bar was full of Western journalists, military officers, aid workers and European officials and a cloud of smoke hung over them as they gossiped together and shared the latest news from the battle hotspots.

Black peered through the crowd, spotted Nick Rowe,

and beckoned him over.

Ex-SAS and now working for 14 Intelligence Company or The Det, as it was known, Nick Rowe was the archetypal grey man. Trained to provide deep surveillance, everything Nick saw told him something. He was an expert in observation and he was tasked with providing the detail the American spy satellites couldn't unearth.

'Aren't we a bit exposed here?' he asked as Black relaxed into one of the chairs in the centre of the hotel lobby.

'Well, I'm not sitting in there,' Black replied in disgust. 'Anyway, I may be posing as a Foreign Office diplomat but everyone knows I am MI6. So, what have you got for me?'

Nick Rowe handed him a photograph.

'I'm watching this man. He's a paramilitary leader in the Kosovan Liberation Army called Spartak Tosca. He smuggles tobacco and uses his military status as a cover for organised crime.'

'Yes, yes, I'm getting bored. I'm not bothered about a petty Kosovan criminal. Both sides have committed atrocities, but the Serbs have committed more and they were the aggressors. You can see how it will pan out. The Kosovans have the world media on their side so the West cannot allow the Serbs to win. The Americans will use their spy satellites to monitor the Serbian army and then they will contain them with precision bombing. Then we can all go home.'

Black was tetchy. He was still thinking about Lord Granville.

'There is more to it than that. Spartak is preparing the logistics to get his products into Europe and his wealth out of the country.' Nick passed Black a GCHQ transcript. 'He's talking to this man in northern Cyprus,' he said, handing Black a photograph.

Black scanned the documents and suddenly his attitude changed. Nick continued:

'The funny thing is the man in northern Cyprus is talking to a man in Leeds. He seems to be plotting some sort of revenge on this chap who is a local solicitor in Harrogate.' Nick pointed at one of the names.

Black stared at the names on the paper with an excited disbelief. Like someone trying to comprehend that they had just won the lottery.

'Does this make any sense to you?' Nick asked eventually, in frustration at Black's silence.

'Oh, it makes perfect sense,' Black replied, giving Nick a smile like a cat that got the cream. 'You're getting through to me loud and clear.'

The sound of drumming was loud. Surprisingly loud. Ian stopped and looked up at the tree canopy. Sky stopped and looked up at Ian wondering why he had stopped.

It was a great spotted woodpecker pecking at the top of a tree. It was hard to believe that something so small could make so much noise. It was also hard to spot, but eventually its red plumage caught Ian's eye.

The common misconception was that they were drilling holes, but this bird was staking out its territory. Letting all the other woodpeckers in the area know that this was his parish.

Ian carried on across The Stray towards the office, the sound still reverberating far and wide. Like marching to a military beat, in rhythm, he recalibrated, and his blood pressure lowered. What would the day bring? He hoped his battles would be easy.

'What's wrong?' Ian asked as soon as he saw Holly. He could see she was upset.

'Which do you want first? The sad news or the bad news?'

'The sad news,' Ian replied.

'Roly Pound has died,' she said, her eyes filling with tears.

'No, he can't have!' Ian exclaimed. 'He only signed his will a couple of weeks ago. What did he die of?'

'Old age, apparently. Mrs Carr telephoned and said he sat down in his armchair, went to sleep and never woke up.'

Ian shook his head and looked at his feet. 'Well, it's not a bad way to go I suppose, but it's still a shock. What's the bad news?'

'Graham Towers has been on. He was incandescent! The hunt has been across his land again. Well, the dogs have.'

'What! I can't believe they could be so stupid. I warned them of the consequences.' Ian was pacing up and down, his voice rising with every statement.

'I know and he wants another home visit. He asked me to get you to ring him as soon as you got in.'

'Okay, well let me ring Major Urquhart first and I will see what is going on,' Ian said, starting to calm down. 'Any chance of a coffee?'

'Of course.'

Holly made her way to the kitchen as Ian flung the Crombie over a spare chair and reached for the telephone. Ed stopped what he was doing to listen in.

'Major Urquhart here,' the Major boomed when he answered the telephone.

'Hello, this is Ian Sutherland from Sutherland Solicitors. I wrote to you on behalf of my client, Graham Towers, a few weeks ago regarding trespass across his land and you replied saying it wouldn't happen again.'

'Yes.'

'Well, it has.'

'I know. Terribly sorry. The dogs got the scent of a fox and we couldn't stop them. We didn't follow, but we have realised we can't stop the dogs, so we are giving up hunting the whole area. We will lose two days a year just because your client has a key parcel of land. Very poor show.'

'Poor show or not, you are leaving yourself open to litigation and I suspect Mr Tower's pockets are deeper than the yours.'

'Yes, yes, I realise all that. It won't happen again.'

'That's what you said last time.'

'Don't get clever with me laddie. If it's a war you want.'

'You'll lose,' Ian said, cutting the Major off before he could finish. Both paused for breath, then the Major continued.

'Look, it's the end of the season and we simply won't include Tower's land and the surrounding area in our fixture list for next year.'

'Can you put that in writing to me please and, in the meantime, I will try to pacify Mr Towers.' Ian said, now playing the role of the good cop.

'Will do,' the Major replied, as though acknowledging an order.

Ian drank his coffee and braced himself to telephone Graham Towers. Surprisingly, his temper had cooled and he accepted Ian's suggestion that there would be no point going for an Injunction at the end of the season if the hunt was not going to be active in the area the following year.

'I still want to see you, though,' Graham said. 'Can

you come now?'

'I've got an urgent letter to do first, but I could come this afternoon.' Ian replied.

'That'll do. I'll be in all afternoon.'

Ian picked up his Dictaphone and started dictating a letter to Philip Jennings. Ian apologised for making contact 'out of the blue' but informed him he was a beneficiary under the will of Roly Pound and Ian explained the reasoning behind Roly's thinking. He gave a conservative estimate of the value of the estate and asked Mr Jennings to make contact as soon as possible.

'I think we should just send this 'care of' to the address we have for Margo Jennings,' Ian said as he passed the tape to Holly. 'If we contact her first, it will only delay things and she will end up knowing some of the story before Philip, which isn't quite right, as he is the main beneficiary.'

'Makes sense to me boss,' Holly replied obligingly.

When Ian arrived at Middle Wood Farm, Graham Towers was on the drive packing some items into the back of the Shogun.

'Hop in lad,' he said, opening the passenger door for Ian and removing some minor items. 'I want to show you my property portfolio.'

Graham had a shock of white hair and looked to be in his late fifties. He was physically strong with a barrel-shaped chest, but as he got into the Shogun, Ian could see Graham's hip was causing him some pain.

'I told you, when we got married, I had nothing but a ten-shilling note in my back pocket.' Ian nodded and Graham continued.

'I worked on a building site every hour God sent. Barring winter, I would get there at 6am and never left before 6pm. After a year, I bought my first plot of land and built a house on it, which I sold, even though Kath and I were still living in rented accommodation. The next year I built four and it just went on from there.'

'Very good,' Ian said.

'Building is cyclical. Feast and famine. You have a few good years and then a few bad. I saved my money and now I never have any less than a million pounds on deposit.'

'Do you have any shares?' Ian asked.

'No. Too risky. But when things are bad, I buy more property, especially from the cowboys who have overstretched themselves. I do them up and sell them on but if they won't sell, I keep them and rent them out.'

'Interesting,' Ian said, thinking that such a strategy would result in a portfolio of undesirable properties.

'Now I own 20.' They were passing through the village of Coxwold at this point and Graham suddenly said: 'I own that one there.' It was a pretty cottage.

'What are the rest of the properties like?' Ian asked.

'That's what I'm about to show you!' Graham replied, giving Ian a kindly smile.

They came into the village of Sowerby and Graham slowed down.

'I bought that one,' he said, pointing to a large house on Front Street overlooking the green, 'and then I built another one in the back garden with access on to Back Lane.'

Ian felt he was meant to be impressed, but it wasn't exactly rocket science. Graham was clearly astute though.

Graham turned left into Gravel Hole Lane. 'I own all those,' he said, referring to a terrace of four properties. They were redbrick with pantile rooves and upvc windows.

'Do you have a letting agent looking after these?' Ian queried.

'What and pay them 10% or more? Do you think I'm stupid?'

'How do you find tenants then and what do you do about tenancy agreements?'

'I'm going to talk to you about all that,' Graham teased, obviously wanting to keep Ian waiting.

Graham then took a right at the end of the lane and drove past the school before pulling up on South Crescent.

'I own all those,' he said, sweeping his hand in an arc behind him, 'and that house, I turned into flats,' he indicated, pointing at a large, square, ugly building.

'So, what is it you want from me?' Ian asked.

'Kath heard you on radio York, that legal Eagle programme talking about wills.'

'Oh, yes. I was interviewed for Will Aid last November. Do you want a will?'

'No, I don't. I'm not tempting fate.'

'Making a will won't make you die any sooner,' Ian said, trying to reassure him.

'Well, I'm not so sure about that and I definitely don't want one,' Graham replied firmly.

Ian's mind flashed back to Roly Pound who had died suddenly after making his will, but perhaps he had just sensed that the end was near. People do get an inkling when their time is up, Ian thought to himself.

'Well, how can I help you?' Ian asked.

'We used Daltons in Thirsk until now, but you will have heard about their problems, so I want you to take over. Anything I buy or sell; you can do it.'

Ian wouldn't normally poach another solicitor's client, but Daltons had been closed down by The Law Society for client account irregularities.

'That's very kind of you, but how do you find your tenants and what do you do about tenancy agreements?' Ian persisted.

'Word of mouth. In the pub mainly! Kath helps me with the business, paperwork and the like, so we eat out regularly. Just bar meals,' he added hastily. 'You can do tenancy agreements for the better village properties, but this lot aren't worth it,' Graham said, making another broad gesture with his arm.

'If you have a troublesome tenant and you haven't got a tenancy agreement, you haven't got a legal leg to stand on,' Ian cautioned.

'The sort of tenants I have aren't worth suing. This is all they understand.' Graham lifted the central arm rest in the Shogun between the two front seats to reveal a plastic tray containing a few coins and a pack of mints. He removed this to divulge a stash of cash hidden underneath. Rolled £20 notes all neatly bundled with rubber bands and packed next to each other like soldiers standing to attention. Ian had no idea how much it amounted to but it must have been, at least, £10,000.

'Are you telling me you don't declare this?' Ian asked instinctively.

'If you grant short term tenancies, the Inland Revenue expect you to let a property for 10 months out of every 12 and if you have a portfolio of properties, they would expect a 10% vacancy rate. I do better than that so I just do a bit of skimming, that's all.'

'There seems to be a lot of cash in there,' Ian countered.

Graham let out a long sigh indicating he was getting bored of having to justify himself.

'The better properties we put through the books. Like that one in Coxwold is let to a pilot and he pays by standing order, but this lot are let to work-shy benefit claimants.

They come and go and I collect the cash regularly, in small amounts. That's the way to deal with them and if they don't pay, I bring a few of my brickies round and we get rid of them.'

'That's a criminal offence! You could be prosecuted under the Protection from Eviction Act,' Ian replied, becoming more exasperated by the minute.

'These sorts of people don't want to get mixed up with the law,' Graham parried, looking unperturbed.

Ian shuffled in his seat. 'I can act for you if you buy or sell something, but I can't get involved with the cash and I can't take payments in cash. I'd be done for money laundering.'

Graham laughed. 'I don't want you to bank the cash. I do that in Switzerland.'

'How do you do that?' Ian asked and immediately regretted that he had done so.

'Me and Kath have a holiday once a year. We drive to Zurich and just pay in the cash. I have a numbered bank account.'

Ian shook his head in disbelief or, rather, disappointment. He had thought Graham's success was based on hard work and shrewd investment but, the truth was, it was tax evasion that gave him the advantage.

'What?' Graham asked.

'Oh, nothing,' Ian said. 'It just seems overly complex.'

'Look lad. I don't want to get you into any trouble. I

just want a decent solicitor we can relate to and we like you.'

'Why don't you just declare the cash? Then you can sleep at night.'

'No, I pay enough tax and I sleep just fine!' Graham said, laughing out loud. 'That's why I have a numbered account. It's completely anonymous and the duty of absolute silence is enshrined in Swiss law. They won't reveal the details of my account to any tax authority in the world. That's why people bank in Switzerland.'

'So, if you have a million pounds on deposit and you have enough money for all your needs, what's the point of storing up cash in a Swiss bank account? You can't spend it all in Switzerland and if you bring it back you will have to pay tax on it and interest and a penalty!'

'It's a security blanket and that does help me sleep at night!' Graham said firmly.

'But when you die it will have to be brought back and your estate will have to pay inheritance tax on it, on top of any income tax penalties. Taxes are designed so that if one doesn't catch you another one will.'

'When I die, I won't care. Anyway, we're leaving it all to charity so there won't be any inheritance tax. The RSPCA can have it.'

'Not if you don't do a will they can't.'

Graham laughed again. 'All right lad, I give you full marks for trying. Come on, I'll get you back to that fancy car of yours.'

They drove back, pretty much in silence, Ian looking at the countryside and mulling things over. As he got into his car, however, Graham came over and looked a little more serious.

'I'm having my hip replaced soon,' he said, resting a hand on the vinyl hood and lowering his face so that it was level with Ian's, 'and if anything happens to me, I just want to know you will sort everything out for Kath.'

Ian nodded understandingly. 'I will,' he said, as he started the engine and headed home.

Ian was right that it would be money laundering if he accepted Graham's cash and paid it out again or invested it for him, using his client account to wash it clean of its sins. But that was not Graham's crime. He was simply evading tax.

Tax evasion had many guises. In its simplest form, people paid cash for goods or more usually services to avoid paying VAT. The recipients of this cash then had to spend it in a non-traceable way on small ticket items such as petrol or a meal out.

Graham had taken this to the next level. He was evading income tax, but to such an extent that the cash was becoming a problem. There was too much to spend, so then he had to tackle the issue of what to do with it and he was certainly storing up problems for the future.

Corporations also evaded tax and employed highly paid professionals to help them. This, in some way, helped legitimise it in the minds of the perpetrators, but the renovations to business premises which were really for a new kitchen at home, the personal assistant who was really an au pair or the company pool car which was used solely by one director, were all variations of putting cash in the back pocket. Then there were the more sophisticated constructions. Tax relief for research the cost of which was exaggerated and profits switched to lower tax jurisdictions via management charges for services which were not provided, all encouraged the attitude of: 'if they can get away with it why shouldn't we?'

However, none of this was money laundering. Money laundering was carried out by professional criminals who would take illicit cash and clean it in a variety of ways so that it could be spent on real assets, unlike Graham's money which was hidden away never to see the light of day.

Enablers and facilitators claim it is a victimless crime, but the cash comes from activities such as drug trafficking, human trafficking, and illicit trade. All in all, the International Monetary Fund estimates that money laundering equates to approximately 5% of the world's gross domestic product every year, placing that much of a greater burden on the honest taxpayers.

Frederick Granville was an expert in such matters and

he had just arranged a meeting which would bring all his plans together. Plans which included Ian being arrested for money laundering, being struck off the solicitors' roll and spending at least five years in prison. He wanted Ian to lose his livelihood and his reputation, but, most of all, he wanted Ian to suffer.

Chapter Three

Spring 1999

Ian was feeling tired. It had been a hard winter and, although the days were lighter, it was still cold. He needed some respite, so he rose early and, grabbing a newspaper, decided to treat himself to breakfast at Bettys.

He ordered a cafetière of Kenyan single origin coffee and, reliving a childhood memory, granary toast. It arrived warm and soaked in butter. Perhaps not the healthiest choice, but certainly a comforting one.

Two middle-aged ladies were sat at an adjacent table talking loudly about their daughters, both of whom had just moved to Chelsea apparently. Ian wasn't trying to listen, in fact, he was trying not to as he flicked over the pages of the newspaper and shook his head in dismay. The war in Kosovo had made the headlines, again. Truce negotiations taking place in Rambouillet, France, had broken down when the Serbian delegation refused to sign the treaty, so NATO had now commenced air strikes on Serbian targets. President Clinton could not risk American lives with boots on the ground, so it was a matter of identifying the targets and obliterating them. The papers had been full of pictures showing streams of refugees walking with whatever they could carry to a place of safety. Now, the pictures were of blown-up buildings and rubble, and onlookers covered in blood and concrete dust, staring in shock.

Suddenly, one of the loud ladies became louder.

'Relationships,' she screeched at the top of her voice. 'It's all about relationships.'

Quite a few people turned around to see what the commotion was about. Ostensibly, one of the daughters had boyfriend problems.

'Time to go,' Ian muttered to himself as he stood up and headed for the office.

It was good to see Holly's smiling face. She was such a positive person. A good appointment, Ian decided.

'Philip Jennings has been on,' she said excitedly.

'Thank God for that,' Ian replied. 'I was getting worried. It's been almost four weeks since we wrote to him.'

'He's coming to see you this afternoon. He said something about only being here for a short time before he had to go abroad again.'

'Great,' Ian replied. 'It will be interesting to see what he's like.'

Early forties, medium build, slightly greying hair, was the

answer. Nothing out of the ordinary, except perhaps, the benevolence of his heart, Ian thought later.

'Hello,' Philip said, shaking Ian's hand. 'I am sorry not to have responded sooner, but I have been delivering clothes to Macedonia.'

'Gosh, I've just been reading about the Balkans. Terrible situation. Do you work for an aid agency?'

'Yes, I work for the Red Cross and we are helping NATO and the United Nations High Commissioner for Refugees establish camps in Macedonia.'

'Sounds a worthy cause. It must be very rewarding?'

'It's very challenging. There are tens of thousands of refugees fleeing Kosovo and that number will most likely increase. The sheer weight of numbers makes it difficult to cope and many of them have suffered terribly. I've just come home for a couple of weeks to organise a collection of clothing from Churches Together.'

'That's very admirable of you,' Ian said. 'Fortune obviously favours the kind!'

'I just feel so guilty,' Philip replied. 'I read your letter and felt like I'd won the lottery, but then I thought this poor old chap has died. Thing is, I didn't know him. I had heard of him from my mother, but only as her friend's husband. That's it.'

'Well, come on through and I will tell you all about Roly Pound.'

Ian and Philip went into the meeting room and Ian took

Philip through the next steps in relation to Roly's estate.

'Firstly, we register the death with all those institutions which Roly had dealings with. Banks, utility companies, that sort of thing. Then, when we have a value for everything, we fill out a tax form and an application for Grant of Probate. That stage probably takes about four weeks. Then, after about another four weeks, the Grant of Probate is issued and that gives the executors the authority to deal with the assets of the estate. So, we can sell the house, if that's what you wish, close the bank accounts and distribute the funds to the beneficiaries in accordance with the terms of the will.'

'What about inheritance tax?' Philip asked.

'There shouldn't be any. The estate is within what we call the nil rate band.'

'Great!' Philip replied, looking pleasantly surprised. He also confirmed he was happy to leave everything in Ian's hands, so Ian wrapped up the meeting and walked Philip back through reception.

'Is it just clothes you are taking to Macedonia?' Ian enquired.

'Yes, for now. We estimate there will be 200,000 people living outdoors in refugee camps and they will be desperate for food, water, shelter, clothing, and medical supplies, but for obvious reasons all we can take in advance is clothes. Food is perishable and medical supplies need a special import licence so we leave all that stuff to the UN.'

Ian looked at his Crombie draped over a chair.
'Is this any good to you?' he asked picking it up.
Philip hesitated and looked a little surprised.
'Well, yes. It still falls below freezing at night.'
'Then take it,' Ian said as he handed him the coat.

The two loud ladies were right. It was all about relationships and not just on a personal level. They were crucial in international affairs as well. History matters and the relationships created in the past affect the future. The sides countries take in a war, the allies they support, affect the movement of people and international trade patterns for decades to come.

For centuries the Balkans were part of the Ottoman Empire, so it was no surprise that when Spartak Toska wanted to expand his Macedonian operations internationally, he headed first for Istanbul and from there on to northern Cyprus.

Frederick Granville pulled up outside a casino near Kyrenia in his Jeep, perfect for the local terrain, and walked through the entrance. He asked for the private members' area and ordered a bottle of Krug champagne. If he was going to pay through the nose for something, he wanted to drink a substance he could trust rather than the local piss.

When Spartak arrived, he paused before entering to admire the doors. There were two sets of double doors decorated like aces from a pack of cards. The ace of diamonds, the ace of hearts and so on. He entered through the door embossed with the ace of spades.

Granville stood up when he saw him. Spartak towered over him. He was six foot four, had grey hair and was well built. He had a neatly trimmed grey beard and thick black eyebrows. He was probably around fifty, and his size and dark features gave him an intimidating physical presence, emphasized by the two bodyguards that stood like bookends beside him.

A waitress came over and offered to take his tan shearling coat which would have made him look like a second-hand car salesman if his demeanour wasn't so menacing.

'No,' he said, turning his shoulder away from her.

Granville indicated he should sit down on a large leather armchair and poured him a glass of champagne. He topped up his own glass and sat down to the side of him, but at an angle so they sat like two politicians posing for the cameras. The two bodyguards remained standing at the entrance to the private area and provided their only real audience.

'So, you said you would like to invest some money with me?' Granville began.

Spartak nodded, stood up and took off his coat. It looked heavy. He sat down again and draped the coat over the low, oblong, glass-topped table in front of them.

'How much would you like to invest?' Granville asked, pressing him gently.

'One million dollars. To start. There will be more.' Spartak spoke with a heavy, guttural accent.

'And I assume I will receive it in cash?'

Again, Spartak nodded. 'But I am not criminal. I am businessman.'

'I don't care about the crime,' Granville chortled. 'It's the proceeds of crime I'm interested in.'

'Business. The proceeds of business. I have cigarette factory in Macedonia.'

'Why now?'

'Because this war has wrecked my trade in Yugoslavia – what's left of it is controlled by the Serbs. I am Kosovan. I based my business in Macedonia after the Bosnian war in 1992 but now I must change again. I need new markets.'

'Does your factory make cheap whites or counterfeit brands?'

'We make branded products like Marlboro. They have much higher margin.'

'And how do you intend to cross borders without falling foul of customs?' Granville paused and then added: 'I take it you are wishing to avoid paying tobacco duties?'

'We will start in a small way using mules from the refugee camps and build on the most successful routes from there. Vehicles with false compartments – that sort of thing.'

Granville rubbed his hand across his mouth as he assessed the business plan. 'And how will you bring the cash back?'

Spartak grinned showing a set of surprisingly good teeth. 'The British are very generous. They send us a lot of aid. Who will question a few teddy bears filled with cash?'

Granville shook his head gently. 'Longevity is your problem. I can see it working to start with, but the war won't last forever.'

'Okay, we will roll up the cash, put it in a condom and stick it up the mule's ass. They know what to do.' Spartak was angry now, but Granville raised both hands, palms facing towards Spartak apologetically.

Spartak took a deep breath. 'Entrepreneurs adapt, Mr Frederick. I have had to adapt all my life. My father was a policeman. He was also a violent, adulterous drunk. He deserted me, my mother, and my sisters when I was only 12 years old. From that age, I started supporting my family. We were poor but we survived.'

'What did you do?' Granville asked.

'I became rich, and when I did, I swore I would never be poor again.'

'No, I meant how did you become rich?'

'I knew who my father's enemies were, so I made them my friends. I worked for them and, as a bonus, they beat him up.' Spartak laughed. 'He deserved it. I don't like men who cheat on their wives.'

Granville rubbed his fingers around his collar. Contemplating his own behaviour, he was feeling uncomfortable.

'Anyway, what is it to you?' Spartak continued. 'I just give you the money. You have no risk.'

'That's where you're wrong. Banking is becoming more regulated by the minute and I must be careful even in northern Cyprus. You must know the right people and if I am going to take a risk, it must be for a long-term successful relationship.' Granville paused. 'I am, however, willing to help you.'

'So, tell me. How can you help me?' Spartak asked gruffly.

'I will deposit your cash in my bank in Nicosia. It is called Sevili Bank, after the highest mountain in Kyrenia. It is entirely independent from my Swiss bank. They are separate businesses as the Swiss bank is much more highly regulated – it must verify the source of funds. Here, they are less fussy. Then we will pursue the three Ps.'

'What are these Ps?'

Granville sat back and sipped his champagne. Now he was in his element.

'Firstly, placement. We find a financial institution in Britain, let's say a small firm of lawyers, that has less sophisticated controls and customer onboarding processes than the bigger firms, and we deposit money into their client account. We then find an excuse to ask for it back and, voila, it comes out clean. Any major clearing bank will accept a solicitor's client account cheque without question, but they would be wary of the source of funds from a small bank in northern Cyprus – a place that only Turkey recognises as a sovereign state.'

Spartak was listening carefully.

'Secondly, property. We use the clean funds to buy you property. Whatever you like. A London flat, a country estate, but I would also recommend a business. A cash generative business, like this casino, where we can mix the illicit cash with clean money.'

'I like the sound of this property,' Spartak interrupted.

'Saves the mule's ass and de-risks the situation.' Granville laughed out loud at his own joke.

'And thirdly?'

'I'm still on property. We don't buy it in your name, but in the name of a company. Registered in, let's say, the Cayman Islands. That company can be owned by you or by a Trust registered in Switzerland. My Swiss bank can provide the custodial services and the beneficiaries can be anyone of your choosing. Your wife, children, any member of your family. It can be discretionary so that none of them have a defined benefit and it can all be controlled by you. We do this to keep the identity of the ultimate beneficial owner hidden and if anyone does try to investigate, they will get bogged down in a quagmire of opaque documentation.'

Granville was concerned in case the last bit was getting too intricate, but it is amazing how criminal minds can grasp the most complex of subjects when their basic instincts are aroused.

'I have wife and two teenage daughters. And my sisters. My mother is no more. My wife is six years older.'

'Six years older?' Granville asked in surprise.

'Yes, six years older,' Spartak replied narrowing his eyes. Granville thought it better not to press the matter.

'Well they can all be beneficiaries and the beauty of a discretionary trust is that you get to decide who gets what, according to need.'

'But I keep control?'

'Yes, of course. You have complete control.'

'And thirdly?' Spartak repeated.

'Profit! Thirdly, the result is profit. Profit which you can spend without any worry of repercussions. I don't know, you'll be sending your girls to Roedean next.'

Spartak didn't fully understand this last comment but he got the gist.

'And you know such lawyers? You have the connections?' Spartak queried.

'I have all the right relationships. I have an agent in Leeds who will find a business to launder the cash from the UK cigarette sales and we have a lawyer in mind to clean the money you deposit here.'

'Okay, I will provide you with the cash and you can provide the three Ps,' Spartak said, pushing his coat towards Granville.

'What's this?'

'The deposit. You will find it in the lining. You can keep the coat,' Spartak replied laughing again.

'Do you want me to count it?'

'No, but let me tell you this, Mr Frederick. You speak well and I look forward to our partnership, but if you betray me, you will create a blood feud between us and I will kill you. That is what we do in Kosovo. Do you understand me?'

'Perfectly,' Granville quietly gulped on some champagne trying not to look concerned. 'However, there is one more thing.'

'What?'

'I need your bodyguards. I need them to carry out some operations for me, on the ground, in England, where they will need to liaise with my agent.'

'And what am I meant to do for protection?'

'I can recommend someone. I know this ex-KGB agent living here on the island. Her name is Polina.'

'A woman! Huh! Do you think I am stupid?' Spartak looked at his bodyguards and sniggered as he awaited Granville's answer. His bodyguards grinned sheepishly.

'Don't ridicule the idea. Your men are just thugs. Probably, from the same village as you. Perfect for my needs, but you deserve something better. A woman blends in; these guys stick out like a sore thumb and Polina is trained. Trained by experts in evasive driving, firearms, hand-to-hand combat, and martial arts.'

'What happened to her last client?' Spartak queried.

'He sent her here to avoid arrest. She killed his chef.'

'Why?'

'The chef tried to poison him,' Granville said as he burst out laughing.

'Okay,' Spartak said, nodding his head slowly. 'I need them to move some stock from Kosovo first but, after that, so long as I like Polina, they're all yours. The ugly one's called Granit and the fat one's called Valon.' This time it was Spartak who laughed loudly, but his bodyguards were not amused.

'What's your agent called?'

Granville sat back and mused for a moment. He was thinking of Ian Sutherland and being stuck in prison reading a newspaper article about another family brought to ruin by Sutherland's high-minded principles.

'My friend, the enemy of my enemy,' he whispered to himself, echoing an explanation Spartak had given earlier.

'Pardon?'

'Hayden Boyes,' Granville replied. 'His name is Hayden Boyes.'

Chapter Four

The sound was the first thing that struck him. Like rumbling thunder. But it was the reverberation of rubber tyres on cobbles. Enzo Hasani stopped what he was doing to listen. His heart in his mouth. He could hear screaming and shouting. The racket of people running. Then five members of the PJP (Special Police Units) burst into the supermarket firing their Kalashnikovs in the air. Everyone froze.

They were dressed in black uniforms and wearing balaclavas so they could not be recognised. Enzo knew, however, that these elite police included some of Serbia's most murderous gangsters.

'You have one hour to leave,' one of them said. 'If you are still here when we get back, we will kill you.' Then they left to share their message with the Hasani's neighbours.

Enzo was in no doubt that they would happily implement the Serbian government's policy of ethnic cleansing. He looked at his mother. He was only 21 but, in their culture, he carried much of the responsibility for his family. His father Ervin was just 60, but prematurely aged by Western standards. Small and hunched, a life of hard physical labour had taken its toll. He too looked to his wife for direction.

'Empty the tills, Enzo. Quickly! Then come and help me with the bags.' Leona had also taken the threat seriously. It was time to leave.

Enzo did as he was asked. There were only two tills. It was more of a convenience store really, although the sign outside said: 'Supermarket.'

All their savings were in German Marks, kept in cash, as was the local custom, and Enzo crammed all the Marks from the tills into a plastic wallet. He put on his leather jacket and put the wallet into an inside pocket and closed the zip. The local dinars from the tills, he stuffed into the right front pocket of his jeans.

Their supermarket was in Vushtrri which was about 17 miles northwest of Pristina. A small city of about 26,000 inhabitants with many surrounding agricultural villages.

They feared this day would come and their bags were partly packed already. Passports, family papers, a few photographs, all in place. Enzo ran upstairs and looked at his mother anxiously. His father watched in bewilderment as his mother threw clothes at him with staccato orders regarding what to put where.

They were packing ordinary suitcases. Like the ones you would take to the airport with those little wheels to pull them along the conveyor-belted walkways. Suddenly,

Enzo realised how inappropriate these were to hike across the countryside *en route* to Macedonia.

He grabbed his college rucksack. He felt a panic inside his stomach as he tried to make decisions. He took out the books. What should he take? Socks, boxers, his T-shirts, his washbag. He had nothing else really. Not that he could carry.

His mother had gone downstairs. She was putting food into the suitcases and shouting orders at her husband. Baked beans. Tinned tomatoes. Anything that wouldn't go off.

'Go and find Merita and Leon,' his mother shouted. 'We will meet you down the road,' by which she meant the main road to Pristina. 'And take Blue,' she added. Blue was Leon's gorilla, a soft toy that he was devoted to and which seemed to have gained a special importance within the family.

Leon was only five. Named after his mother, he was her lion cub, the apple of her eye and Rita, as she was known, would be collecting him on her way back from college. She was 16 and wanted to be a lawyer, like Ally McBeal from the TV series of the same name.

Enzo went immediately whilst his parents continued packing. He walked quickly and then trotted against the counter-flow of friends and neighbours, all abandoning their homes and livelihoods to reach the safety of Macedonia. They had been given their marching orders.

'Go to Pristina where a train will take you to Skopje.' They were, literally, fleeing for their lives.

He could see a rush of school children, like a tidal wave coming towards him and, thankfully, Rita had Leon with her. She was encouraging him to hurry and she waved as she saw Enzo approaching. It looked as though the Kosovan Liberation Army were setting up a roadblock, he assumed to slow down the Serbs, but their activity was obstructing the locals as well.

Enzo was wary of the KLA. Some of his relatives had joined and they said it was run by gangsters, just like the PJP. They smuggled drugs, ran prostitution rackets, and murdered civilians, and they were using this war to strengthen their criminal operations. However, at least these gangsters were on his side – supposedly.

At first, Enzo had thought that the KLA were setting up a roadblock, but on closer inspection it seemed they were relieving a warehouse of its cigarettes. Slashing open large cardboard boxes with a Stanley knife and emptying the contents into plastic sacks which they were loading into the back of a pick-up truck. Dozens of bags were piled high.

Rita sighed when she saw who was supervising the loading of the pick-up. It was brothers, Granit and Valon Hoxha, and Valon fancied her.

'Hello, my beauty. Get in the truck and we will give you a lift to safety,' Valon shouted, giving her a toothy smile.

'No thanks,' she replied. 'I've got my brother with me.' She said it a little dismissively.

'There's room for Leon,' Valon persisted. He was at least 10 years older than Rita and his heavy build made an uncomfortable juxtaposition to her petite frame and pretty features.

'No, Enzo is here now,' she said and raised her hand to beckon him closer. Enzo started pushing his way through the throng of people moving in the opposite direction.

'Then let him take Leon,' Valon snarled, grabbing her arm with his left hand as she tried to push past the truck. Enzo saw this and quickened his pace.

'Get off me you pig!' Rita said, trying to pull her arm away but Valon tightened his grip. To him this was quite an insult. She had gone too far. He was a Muslim and many of the Serbian peasants, the enemy, were pig farmers, so it was a double insult. People had heard her. Granit had heard her.

Granit stopped loading and looked at his younger brother to see what he would do next. Valon glared at her.

'You have been promised to me,' he growled, tugging her arm towards him. 'By your father.'

'Not true,' she said, trying to pull her arm away as she looked at him with a piercing glare. 'Anyway, he doesn't own me. I'm going to leave this country and you far behind me.'

The public humiliation was too much. Valon was seething inside. She had belittled him. Kosovan women were meant to know their place, but she was far too spirited with all her modern ideas.

He gave her a cynical smile and scoffed at her remark. Almost as though he had just made a decision and accepted a different future.

'Well, no one else will want you,' he said and then with the Stanley knife, still in his right hand, he slashed at her cheek, cutting her from the bottom of her right eye to the corner of her mouth. Blood spewed from her face and she let out a small scream, as she involuntarily gasped, and held her hand to her cheek. Enzo's stomach twisted as he realised, he hadn't reached her in time. He squeezed through the crowds, using both arms to push his way through, with the desperation of someone drowning.

Valon took a step back, ostensibly surprised by his own actions, as Enzo ran forwards to help his sister. He pulled a T-shirt from his rucksack and gave it to her to hold against the wound. He looked at Valon, contemplating his next step but Valon took a fighting pose, thrusting his right arm forward with the Stanley knife still tightly gripped in his hand, daring Enzo to come forward.

Rita pressed her hand on Enzo's shoulder to restrain him.

'Come on, we have to go,' she said, giving Valon a cold stare of contempt, as she quietly vowed his day would come.

Leon was crying. Enzo grabbed Blue out of the rucksack and handed it to him. Leon hugged the gorilla to his chest as though his life depended on it. Enzo took his hand and dragged him away. 'Come on Leon. We must find Mami and Babi.'

Enzo, Rita, and Leon soon caught up with their parents, uncles, aunts, and cousins. There were 16 in their wider family unit and with friends and neighbours from the same district, about 300 souls making the trek to Pristina. Some had managed to catch a train, but there was a lack of information at Vushtrri station, and the Hasani family were not going to wait around while the PJP were patrolling the area.

It was late afternoon on a Friday and the children were fractious. Many of the elderly were infirm and the journey was slow. Those who had cars had been made to leave them behind along with their homes and most of their possessions.

Enzo reckoned they were barely making two miles an hour following the route of the M2 which ran alongside the Sitnica river. Suddenly, he heard a loud, rhythmic, clanking sound in the distance and he looked at Rita knowing immediately what it was.

'I'll run ahead and have a look,' she said.

Rita set off, before Enzo could stop her, still holding

his T-shirt against her face. She rounded a corner and there it was - a convoy of military vehicles, including a tank with caterpillar tracks, heading towards them from Pristina. She ran back to Enzo without being seen.

'What are we going to do?' she said.

Enzo looked around anxiously. If the convoy caught up with them, they would probably be killed.

To their right was a farm track between two fields and it led to the river, perhaps a little over 400 yards from the road. The riverbank was lined with trees and Enzo thought it was their only place to hide.

'Up here, everyone,' he shouted as he started waving his arms furiously to indicate the direction.

Not many of them realised what was happening and they continued to meander.

'Quickly, quickly,' he shouted as Rita ran to the back of the group to usher them along.

They scrambled for the trees and made it just as the convey rounded the corner, Enzo, and Rita, watching, hoping beyond hope, that they hadn't been seen.

Enzo's aunt sat with her back against a tree and started breast feeding Rina, her baby. Rina was only six months old. Others paused to drink water and rummage through their bags.

The Serbian soldiers were on their way to Vushtrri and in a couple of days, they would make the city infamous. They were on a mission but, from 200 yards away, they had spotted the refugees heading for the trees. An order was given to so some soldiers in a jeep, who peeled off from the convoy, whilst it continued to Vushtrri.

The jeep was coming straight up the track towards them. Enzo and Rita watched not knowing what to do. Then it took a 90 degree turn and one of the soldiers started throwing hand grenades into the woods as they drove along the treeline.

No one was hurt although panic reigned as they crouched for cover behind the trees.

The jeep turned around and made a return run. Enzo's aunt had been slow to move but now she made a dash towards her husband. There was an explosion and she fell to the ground. Her husband ran to help her. He had been hit by shrapnel but he barely noticed. He knelt beside his wife and lifted her up. She was covered in blood and still holding Rina.

'I'm okay,' she said.

Her husband's eyes were searching her, looking for where the blood was coming from. Then he saw the shrapnel in Rina's back. A diagonal wound almost the width of her body. She was dead.

Her father's wound was to the arm and blood was dripping freely to the ground, but he didn't notice as he stared at his daughter in utter disbelief. He felt his heart had been ripped out of him. His wife was wailing uncontrollably but all he could think was, Rina was killed because she was a Muslim and she didn't even know she was a Muslim. She was an innocent baby, killed because of a cultural divide about which she knew nothing. They lived with this cultural divide. They even grew to accept it, but now he saw it in all its futility.

In complete shock, he started walking towards the soldiers in the jeep who had stopped to have a cigarette. No one noticed him set off because they were all gathered around the mother who wouldn't let go of her baby. He had no plan. He just kept muttering to himself: 'She didn't even know she was a Muslim.'

When the soldiers saw him approaching from the woods they shot him – dead.

They quickly finished their cigarettes and, having seen no further movement, left to rejoin the convoy.

Enzo's family unit was now just fourteen. There was no time to bury his uncle. They just laid him with Rina at the foot of a large oak tree and covered them with some branches. Enzo's aunt had to be dragged away, but they promised her they would return as they continued walking, along with everyone else, through the night. They had left Vushtrri in fear, but now an even more sombre mood had descended upon them. The silence of the night shattered only by the scraping of the suitcase wheels on the tarmac and the sobbing of those with broken hearts.

Eventually, they arrived at the railway station in Pristina early on Saturday morning. It was the first day of

May. Serbian police were loading people on to a train. It was a cattle train with no windows and no seats.

Each person was stopped as they boarded the train and forced to hand over their money. Enzo's father said he hadn't got any and received a rifle butt to the side of his head. Then they threw him in a carriage and asked Enzo the same question. He pulled the dinars out of his pocket and handed them over, but the policeman threw them to the ground in disgust, only for one of his colleagues to quickly pick them up. The policeman pulled open Enzo's jacket, unzipped the inside pocked and removed the plastic wallet. Seeing the real money, he smiled and waved them on board, Leon still clutching Blue tightly to his chest and Leona and Rita lifting in the suitcases.

They were packed like sardines in a tin and, when the doors were closed, they were in complete darkness. They hoped they were going to Macedonia but they couldn't be sure. Luckily, the journey only took four hours and when the carriage doors were opened the sign said: 'Skopje.'

When they arrived at the Stenkovec UNHCR camp it was already overcrowded. Thousands of people were lighting fires, cooking food, and preparing children for bed under tarpaulins and flimsy tents. Despite all the international aid, conditions were poor.

Two days later a buzz of excitement ran around the camp. Tony Blair, the British Prime Minister, was about to visit. When he arrived, most people thought he was an American politician and they were disappointed that he stayed for less than 15 minutes, but those who met him said he was sympathetic. Then the rumours started. Perhaps there had been a security issue because that same day Vushtrri secured its place in the history books – as the site of a massacre.

A column of about 1,000 refugees had been travelling in a convoy comprising of more than one hundred tractors and trailers. People from the surrounding villages were crammed on to them. They were fleeing the fighting between the KLA and Serbian forces east of Vushtrri. Serbian police and the paramilitary forces that had killed Rina and her father caught up with them and conducted a mass execution. About one hundred men were killed. Some were only boys.

The Hasanis lived outside for six weeks whilst their future was decided. Surprisingly, the process was easier than they thought. Enzo's father said they wanted to go to the UK because, his father had been a partisan in the Second World War and he didn't like the Germans. All fourteen members of his extended family accepted his choice and their wish was granted.

But what would happen next? They knew nothing other than that they received by word of mouth. Their property had been plundered. Those that were still living had to start again.

Enzo paced around the camp waiting for the green

light to leave and for whatever his mother would produce from the stew pot. They could never return to Kosovo. Even if the Serbs were beaten, the criminal gangs would take over. A determination stirred inside him. They would claim asylum and start again from scratch in the UK where he would make his fortune. He would say Rita had been attacked by the KLA. She had the scars to prove it. He saw Rita as their passport, but she also had her own ideas.

Chapter Five

Light rain and cloud greeted the Hasani family as the aeroplane touched down at Leeds/Bradford airport on the 17 June 1999. The English would call it a dull day. For the Hasani family, it was a blessed relief.

Enzo pulled up the collar on his coat, but undid the buttons so he could reach his passport as he approached Border Control. He looked at the labels again. One said: 'Arthur Bell, Gentleman's Tailor, Ripon,' and the other said: 'Ian Sutherland Lupton.'

With admirable efficiency, they were housed in a council house on Oak Road in Ripon. Within a week, Enzo had accepted a job at a mill in Melmerby, working twelve-hour shifts filling plastic bags with fertiliser and within two weeks, he had opened an account with Barclays Bank. By the third week, he was in Ian's office with Rita, asking Holly for an appointment.

Holly was looking at Enzo in disbelief. Firstly, she thought it strange that he was wearing a coat in summer and secondly, she thought she recognised it. She hurried into the meeting room where Ian was talking to Ed.

'I think you'd better come through,' she said.

Ian followed her back into reception and experienced a similar reaction when he saw the coat. Enzo stuck out his hand.

'Enzo Hasani,' he said, with a deep, but quiet voice. He then pointed at his sister. 'Rita. Her English is better.'

'How can I help you?' Ian asked.

Enzo handed Ian some crumpled papers, A4 in size, but they had been rolled up and kept in his coat pocket.

Ian looked a little bewildered but took the papers and said: 'Come on through.'

Before moving, Enzo replied: 'You are Mr Ian?'

'Erm, yes, I am Ian Sutherland.'

Enzo opened the coat and pointed at the label. 'Ian Sutherland Lupton?'

Ian stared at the label which confirmed it was his coat and not an apparition. 'Oh, I see. No, my name is Ian Sutherland. Lupton was the name of my house at school.'

Enzo nodded and seemed to understand, which was a little bit surprising really.

'How come you have my old coat?' Ian asked.

'Mr Philip from refugee camp. We said we needed lawyer and he recommended you. Then he gave me coat to remember name.'

'Oh, I see. Well, come through and have a seat whilst I look at these.'

Ian started flicking through the papers. There were some estate agent's particulars for an ex-council house for sale on King Edward Road, Ripon. The asking price was £75,000. Ian recognised it. He had acted on it before when the tenant had purchased it from the Council under Margaret Thatcher's Right to Buy scheme. Ian could remember that ten or so years ago it had been valued at £22,000 and the tenant, an old lady, had been given a 60% discount. Her grandson, a taxi driver, paid for it in cash.

'So, you want to buy a house?' Ian asked.

Enzo nodded and Rita sat silently.

There were some more papers underneath. Two sheets of A4 containing closely typed print. Ian started reading.

'This looks like a preliminary mortgage offer. The bank is willing to lend you £50,000?'

'Yes,' Enzo said nodding again.

'So, you must have £25,000 somewhere?'

'Yes.'

'Where is that?'

'In the bank.'

'And where did you get it?'

'From a gorilla,' Enzo replied as he smirked at Rita. Then he became more serious and continued, 'My family is from Vushtrri near Pristina. The Serbs came into our supermarket and gave us one hour to leave. We emptied the tills. The Serbs stole the money from our pockets but our savings were in a toy gorilla.' Enzo gave short answers because he didn't have the vocabulary to give longer ones.

'Gosh, I see,' Ian said as he sat back in his chair and paused. 'At least, I think I do.' Suddenly, the reality of the whole situation was becoming apparent to him. He carried on reading, but stopped abruptly.

'According to this, the mortgage term is only for five years? You will have to pay the money back over five years.

'Yes.'

'How will you do that?' Ian asked, never having seen a five-year mortgage term before. Enzo gave him a fixed look.

'I don't drink, I don't smoke, I have no woman until I can provide home.'

Ian sat back in his chair again and gave a warm-hearted smile. It was time to take Enzo seriously.

'Okay, I will telephone the estate agents and let them know that I am acting for you, and I will do the same with the bank. You will need to confirm to them that I am your solicitor,' Ian said, handing over a couple of his business cards.

Enzo looked at Rita and passed her the cards. Then, as he stood up to leave, he pointed at her face.

'The KLA did this. It is dangerous for us in Kosovo.'

Ian looked at Rita's cheek. The scar was about two millimetres wide and it ran down the entire righthand side of her face.

'I hadn't noticed,' he said kindly. It was the truth. Ian

had been concentrating on Enzo but to Rita the words were important. On the one hand she felt lucky to be alive and she was optimistic about the opportunities this new country could provide, but on the other hand she hadn't even started to come to terms with her disfigurement. She had been pretty and now she felt she was ugly, but Ian hadn't even noticed her scar. She decided she liked him. Maybe it wasn't as bad as she thought?

Ryan Curtis dropped his two daughters off at Queen Mary's in the village of Topcliffe and watched as they lowered themselves out of the white BMW X5 and ran into the main school building. With its tall pillars and classical architecture, offset by its beautiful parkland setting, it exuded a stately power.

He delighted in their privileged education but, as he lit a cigarette, he brooded over the irony of how it was paid for.

His heart always sank on the journey to work. The first bit was okay, down the A1 and through Collingham and Bardsey on the A58, but as he turned off what he called the hotel roundabout, into Seacroft, his mood darkened, even if he was only subconsciously aware of it.

Seacroft was home to the second largest council housing estate in the whole of the UK and as he drove past the tall tower blocks, monuments to the socialist housing policies of the seventies, he could not help but be depressed by the cloudy skies, grey concrete, dilapidation, dereliction and deprivation.

He pulled up at the back of his betting shop and entered by way of the back door. The BMW was partially blocking the rear service road to the row of shops rented from Leeds City Council. His betting shop was the end one, but he had several good reasons to park there. The car obstructed others entering through the back door and he could get back into it quickly if necessary. He could also keep an eye on his car through the bar-protected, double-glazed glass and if anyone did complain, such as the refuse collectors, he slipped them a few quid.

The irony was that in this hotspot for the unemployed, those who lived on benefits and drugs, home to prostitutes and petty criminals, in this melting pot of despair, sat the most profitable betting shop in the whole of Leeds. On average, it turned over £15,000 per week and made a net profit of around £3,000.

The problem was, it was never quite enough. Ryan was on his second wife, this one younger and more attractive than the first, but requiring expenditure on hair, nails, designer clothes, gym membership and an open-topped Mercedes. Add in school fees and ponies, and the cost of maintaining a showhouse in Sharow, and you could almost feel sorry for him.

There was also the mental side of things. He was 45, grey haired, nervy and he smoked even though he wished he didn't. He never exercised and had to spend six days a week in his airless back office, bored, just to make sure the cashiers didn't place a few bets for themselves, after the winners had been announced. It was uncanny how lucky punters were if he had a day off.

Twenty-five years ago, he had worked in the betting shop during his summer holidays and proved himself adept at settling bets. Foolishly, he never completed his degree at Leeds University. The money was too good. Then when the founding owner retired, he bought the business by paying over the following year's profits whilst his mentor cruised around the Caribbean. Now this profitable business was his and he was deeply unhappy.

So, Ryan Curtis was not immediately dismissive when Wendy, one of the cashiers, said to him that there were two men in the shop wanting to talk to him about a business proposition.

Ryan stuck his head around his office door and took a peek at Granit and Valon loitering in front of the TV screens. They did not look like businessmen and he was suspicious.

'I will have a word with them, but keep your eyes open and at the first sign of trouble call the police,' he instructed her.

Ryan went out to meet them and sat on one of the tall stools that lined a central counter where the punters wrote out their betting slips, and he indicated to Granit and

Valon that they should do the same. He quickly realised that they were foreign and that their English was poor. Clearly, therefore, they were working for someone else.

'We have business proposition,' Granit said, in his thick accent, as he took out a typed card and read from it.

'We give you £10,000 cash every month. You put through business as losing bets. You must pay betting tax of £675. We send you invoice from legitimate business for security services for £6,000 every month and we charge you VAT of £1,050. You keep £2,275 every month.'

Granit then passed Ryan the card. He looked at it briefly. It was like settling a bet. The figures were correct. They were also generous. Too generous, if truth be known, but Granville wanted to guarantee a positive response from his fall guy. A mark that had been identified for him by Hayden Boyes.

'Why would you do that?' Ryan asked.

'We need clean money,' Granit replied.

Well at least they are honest, Ryan thought to himself before smirking at the irony of his own deliberations.

'I don't know,' Ryan said hesitating.

Granit handed him an off-white, cloth bag with a drawstring top, stood up and both brothers headed for the exit, Granit turning as he left to give a message with his eyes. It was a sort of don't argue with us look and there wasn't really time for Ryan to object. He was left holding the bag.

He went back into his office, opened the bag and counted the money. £10,000 in used notes. Wendy had watched everything so he told her what they had said, realising her silence would also cost him a few quid.

'Well, I suppose I will have to go along with it for now,' he said, 'and a couple of extra grand a month is always helpful.'

'Why not?' Wendy replied. 'They give you the cash first, so what can go wrong?'

Holly gave Ian a mischievous smile when he returned from lunch. Even though she was 30, it was a happy smile from someone who was excited.

'You've got a swear coming in a few minutes,' she said. 'Someone called Nick Rowe.'

Now Ian understood. She was anticipating a treat.

'A swear,' as she called it, referred to a document which had to be signed in front of a solicitor, acting as a Commissioner for Oaths, who then asked the declarant to make an oath confirming that the contents of the document were true. The solicitor then witnessed the document and charged a fee of £5. If any additional documents were attached to the declaration, a further £2 was charged for each, and there was usually, at least, one.

The solicitor was acting as an Officer of the Court, so the charge was a sort of court fee, usually paid in cash and most solicitors pocketed it as beer money. Ian kept a record of these fees, usually about £500 per annum, and declared them on his tax return, but he gave the cash to Holly to buy cakes from Bettys – hence her anticipated delight.

Nick Rowe gave Holly a friendly smile when he arrived and Ian came through to greet him. There was nothing distinguishable about his looks. He was of medium height and build with dark hair, but he did have an air of confidence about him. Not cockiness but a relaxed self-assurance.

They sat down either side of Ian's desk and Nick handed over the papers. It was an affidavit with one exhibit, prepared for the purposes of divorce.

Ian scanned the affidavit. He didn't need to know the details but he did notice the address. It referred to an army barracks at Credenhill, near Hereford.

'Not SAS, are you?' Ian asked, realising the address was home to the special forces.

It was a cheeky question and Ian was expecting an evasive answer, but to his surprise Nick said: 'Yes.'

'Well, I was,' he continued, 'but now I'm in 14 Company.'

'What's that?' Ian asked. 'I've never heard of it.'

'Good! It's a special forces unit established to carry out surveillance operations in Northern Ireland. I am the archetypal grey man that blends into the background, working undercover and feeding back information.'

'Wow,' Ian said, looking both surprised and excitedly interested. He wanted to ask another question but wasn't sure if he should.

'What sort of things do you do, if you don't mind me asking?' he queried hesitantly.

'Well, I might, for example, monitor the amount of fertiliser being purchased by a farmer, hide in a hedge to record what he's doing with it and then, if appropriate, call in a strike.'

'Fertiliser?' Ian asked.

'Yes. It can be used to make explosives.'

'Oh, I see,' Ian said as the penny dropped. 'So, what brings you here?'

'Our Irish gig got kicked into touch by The Good Friday Agreement so I've been supporting NATO in Yugoslavia, gathering information about suspected war criminals. Now, I am on a special assignment here, so I am kipping with 38 Engineer Regiment in Ripon.'

Ian felt he had asked too much and was surprised to have been indulged so he didn't want to push his luck.

'That's fascinating! I'd love to hear more, but I suppose we should get this signed,' Ian said, pointing to the appropriate place on the form.

Nick scribbled his signature and slid the affidavit back round to Ian.

'Now, if you would like to take this Bible in your right hand and repeat after me: I swear by almighty God.'

'I swear by almighty God.'

'That this is my name and handwriting.'

'That this is my name and handwriting.'

'And the contents of this, my affidavit.'

'And the contents of this, my affidavit.'

'Are true.'

'Are true.'

'And this is the exhibit referred to.'

'And this is the exhibit referred to.'

'That's it,' Ian said, as he started to witness the affidavit and mark the exhibit.

'Phew,' Nick replied, as he let out a deep sigh. 'This feels more like getting married than divorced!'

Ian showed Nick back through reception to the exit, shook hands and said good-bye. Then he turned to Holly and handed over the cash.

'That was strange,' Ian said.

'Why?' Holly asked, raising her eyebrows.

'Well, he's ex-SAS and he now works for an undercover unit called 14 Company. I thought that sort of thing was meant to be secret, but he told me all about it.'

'How exciting!' Holly said gleefully.

'Well, don't you tell anyone. I probably shouldn't have told you.'

'No I won't,' she replied.

The next morning Nick was back.

'I've got another affidavit to swear,' he said to Holly. 'Something to do with the financial arrangements this time.'

'Oh, I will just see if Mr Sutherland is free. I'm sure he will fit you in.'

Ian came through and took Nick back to his desk. They sat opposite each other and Ian started flicking through the papers.

'I saw you walking your dog in Studley Roger last night,' Nick ventured.

'Oh, I didn't see you,' Ian replied. Nick just smiled making Ian feel a little bit uncomfortable.

'I live there and go running in the park whenever I can. It's a fabulous asset right on my doorstep.'

'Yes, I'd like to get to know it a bit better. Maybe we could go on a run together and you could show me some of the best routes?'

Ian had slightly mixed feelings. His reluctance to accept the offer was outweighed by the complimentary assumption that he would be fit enough to go on a run with a member of the special forces.

'Okay. When would you like to go?'

'Is tomorrow at 6pm any good for you?'

'Yes, that works for me,' Ian replied, before interrupting his flow to complete the swear.

'Look, I'm sorry if I asked you too many questions yesterday.'

'Not at all. I know all about client/attorney privilege.'

'But you're not a client,' Ian replied, a little anxiously. 'I am acting as an Officer of the Court, not your lawyer.'

'Oh dear,' Nick said, laughing and looking completely unruffled. 'Well, don't tell anyone.' He stood up to leave. 'I'll see myself out, but between you and me, I am watching some Kosovan refugees who are smuggling tobacco. They are ex-KLA and they work for someone we suspect of war crimes.' Nick moved a few steps closer to the exit. 'I just thought you ought to be aware,' he said, as he turned to leave.

Ian watched him go with his mouth hanging slightly open.

'You look as though you've seen a ghost,' Holly said as he turned to face her.

'I'm just a bit surprised about how much he is telling me,' Ian replied.

Holly shrugged. 'Well, we all need someone to talk to. Maybe he has a lot on his shoulders.'

'Maybe,' Ian responded slowly, obviously still processing the situation.

He was right to question things. Nick's divorce was genuine enough. A fortunate coincidence was how Simon Black described it. But Nick's choice of solicitor – there was nothing accidental about that at all.

Chapter Six

Summer 1999

Graham Towers heaved himself into the passenger seat of the Shogun, held on to the grip handle and gave Kath instructions to drive.

He hated being driven, but he had just had his right hip replaced, so he couldn't risk having to do an emergency stop. The constant grinding pain of bone on bone had gone, but he was still very sore as it was only two days since the operation.

Kath drove him to a building site in the village of Baldersby where he had a small infill development of three houses. He expected to see his men working, but all four of them were sat around smoking and drinking tea.

It was 10.30am and they were due a break, but he paid his men well and worked them hard. He was annoyed because he expected them to be working and he knew the only reason they weren't was because he wasn't there to watch them.

The men stood up as soon as they saw his car and started gathering their paraphernalia. One threw away the last of his tea and screwed the lid back on his flask, whilst another quickly stubbed out his cigarette.

'What are you doing you lazy buggers?' Graham shouted as he got out of the car. 'You should be working.'

'Just having a quick break,' the foreman replied.

He wasn't much of a supervisor; he was just the longest serving employee and he had only worked for Graham for three years. Despite the good pay, people just couldn't take the pace.

'Break, my arse! You've probably been sitting around all morning.'

'No, we were just talking about the trench we've dug for the sewage pipe,' the foreman said, leading Graham towards the far end of it. 'There's a problem.'

Graham looked down into the trench and then bent down on one knee. It was a bad movement to make just after a hip replacement and he groaned with pain – something which was unusual for him, especially in front of his workmen. One of the younger men, a Geordie, with a cigarette hanging out of his mouth, lowered himself into the trench and started scraping away some of the soil with his hand.

'It looks like a mosaic floor,' he said.

Graham looked at the small patterned tiles and spat out the words: 'Roman remains,' his voice heavy with loathing.

'You'll have to notify the County Council,' the Geordie

said with some satisfaction whilst exhaling smoke which drifted over Graham.

'Well, I'm not paying for you lot to sit around,' Graham snarled whilst allowing the foreman to help him back to his feet. 'You can put up the boundary fencing and put that disgusting thing out.'

'Sorry. I'm trying to give up, but these were half price in the pub.'

Like many, the Geordie couldn't resist a bargain, but at half price, Spartak was still making a huge margin. Tax made up 80% of the £4 cost price of a packet of cigarettes which meant the pre-tax sale price would be 80p. If they were genuine Marlboro and the cost of production was half the pre-tax sale price, Spartak would be making something for 40p and selling it for £2. However, Spartak's cigarettes cost a lot less than 40p a pack to make. This was because he utilised cheap labour in his factory in Macedonia where there were no regulations so long as he greased the right palms. The Geordie thought he was getting a good deal, but if he realised that a chemical analysis on behalf of Interpol had revealed that the cigarettes contained asbestos, mould, dust, dead flies, rat droppings and even human excrement, he might not consider they were such a bargain.

Granit parked their Mercedes 190 outside an indoor shopping arcade, left Valon to guard it and walked down the row of shops to the betting office. It was a testament to Seacroft that even a Kosovan thug thought it dangerous to leave his car unattended.

He grunted something at one of the cashiers and Ryan Curtis came out to meet him. Granit handed him a cloth bag like the one he had used previously.

'We give you £20,000 this time. Business is good,' he grinned, revealing that his formative years had not included a relationship with an orthodontist.

Ryan sucked in some air through gritted teeth.

'Customs and Excise might get suspicious about this sudden increase in turnover. Statistically, it is incredibly stable at around £60,000 a month. Now I will be turning over £80,000.'

Granit just shrugged and took a crumpled piece of paper out of the back pocket of his jeans. It had a telephone number written on it.

'Boss wants you to ring him,' he said and then he left.

Ryan realised it was an international number, but he didn't bother to look up where it was. He just went into the back office and dialled the number. Frederick Granville answered the phone.

'Hello.'

'This is Ryan Curtis.'

'Ah, thank you for ringing. I'm Freddie.' That was what he called himself nowadays to most people. It was a curious, but quite common phenomenon for white-collar criminals to become less formal after serving time in prison.

'Freddie who?'

'Well, let's just stick with Freddie, shall we? Firstly, thank you for looking after Granit's little problem. He says you've been most helpful.'

Ryan was bemused. He doubted Granit had said anything and started to sense he was dealing with a posh criminal. His mind started to run away with him. A city gent done for a financial crime now living in Spain, he thought.

'And secondly?' Ryan asked.

'Secondly, I would like to buy you a flat. Actually, it's a penthouse apartment in Kensington. It's a new build just off Vicarage Gate, overlooking Kensington Palace Gardens. Lovely.'

'And why would you do that?' Ryan asked sarcastically.

'Well, it's not really for you. It's a short-term thing. You can use it for a while. Take your wife to London for the weekend, but basically, you will be a sort of trustee. I've given your details to the estate agents and I've chosen a solicitor for you in Harrogate which should be convenient. Sutherland Solicitors, they're called.'

'Why me? Why should I have the benefit of all your attention?'

'Oh, I've done my research. You're well suited for the job,' Freddie replied, a little menacingly.

Ryan was silent. He was worried about what he was getting into, but he wasn't sure how to get out and the money was useful.

'Two more things. You must never mention me to anyone. As far as the estate agents and lawyers are concerned, you are the principal client.'

'And the second?'

'Yes, I forgot to mention; it's costing £6,000,000. The stamp duty on that at 3.5% is £210,000. Ask the solicitor, he's called Ian Sutherland by the way, if there is any way you can reduce it by paying a bit in cash.' Freddie paused as Ryan whistled.

'I will send you a cheque for the deposit of £600,000 payable to Sutherland Solicitors. It will be drawn on my bank in northern Cyprus, Sevili Bank. If he questions it, say it's a gift from an uncle or something. Be inventive.'

Freddie put the phone down and Ryan sat in stunned silence. There was very little truth in what Granville had told him. He had no intention of completing the purchase. He couldn't afford to. He was using Spartak's money for the deposit and the stamp duty ruse was just a test to see how far Sutherland could be pushed.

'Time for a Raki,' he said to himself. He swirled the ice and watched his drink go cloudy. Boyes had chosen well. He almost felt sorry for Curtis. In this murky underworld he was just a pawn. Sutherland was the target.

Ian waited for Nick Rowe under the archway in Studley Royal deer park and looked down the straight road towards Ripon Cathedral. It made a beautiful picture in the early evening as the sun got ready for bed.

Ian was apprehensive. There had been a touch of bravado about his acceptance of Nick's offer and now he was worried he would not be up to it.

Ian was watching and waiting for Nick to run up the drive towards him, but silently he appeared from Ian's left, having taken a footpath that ran a little further north, out of the village and into the park.

'Hello,' Nick said with a beaming smile.

'Hello,' Ian replied, nervously.

'So, you want to go on an SAS training run, do you?' Nick asked, teasingly.

'I'll give it a go,' Ian responded tentatively.

'Okay, well let's make this the rendezvous point, shall we?'

Ian looked confused.

'The finish. We'll call it a day when we get back here,' Nick clarified.

'How far are we going?' Ian asked.

'That depends,' Nick replied as he started running back towards the village.

Ian followed and to start with he was pleasantly surprised. For some reason he thought Nick would be too fast for him, but the pace was steady and comfortable, as they ran east, out of the village, along a footpath towards Ripon. They then headed south and Nick stopped at a little footbridge over the river Skell, just before a parkland area called Hell Wath.

'The river's dropped,' Nick said.

Ian looked, but didn't notice anything.

'How do you know?' he asked.

'Look at the stones. They're still wet, but no longer covered by water.'

Before Ian could take a proper look, Nick was off again and at the end of Hell Wath Lane, he turned right up Whitcliffe Lane. This stretch had a gentle, uphill gradient and Nick started putting on some pace. Ian matched him, but it was no longer comfortable.

Ian guessed the route. He reckoned Nick was going to go up to Whitcliffe Hall Farm and then back along the seven bridges. He was wrong.

Nick did take the predicted route for a while, up to the farm, across some fields and then into the woods where he ran down a steep, stony embankment, sideways, to give more grip against the sliding stones underneath.

They paused near a footbridge with green painted iron railings. Ian relaxed thinking it was only about a mile to the archway and it hadn't been as tough as he feared, but Nick turned to face back up the steep stone track with woods on either side.

'Let's pretend there are snipers in these woods. We've

got to reach the top as quickly as possible.'

With that, he shot up the hill, darting from side to side as he aimed for the pinnacle. Ian sprinted after him, following the same zigzag route. It could only have been about 200 yards, if that, but the steep incline sapped the strength from his quads and the last few yards were agony.

'Keep going,' Nick shouted as Ian reached the brow of the hill, gasping for breath, his thighs about to explode.

Nick reached down and picked up two stones about the size of tennis balls as Ian sucked in the oxygen.

'Here, one in each hand,' he said.

'What for?' Ian spluttered as he caught his breath.

'They will strengthen your biceps which helps if you have to carry a weapon,' Nick said, as he set off again.

They continued uphill, still in the woods, until they came into some open fields.

'Ah, we are going to re-join the seven bridges track,' Ian said under his breath, but Nick kept heading west on a slight diagonal towards some more trees.

Ian had thought the stones were light when he had started carrying them but now, they were heavy and his arms ached with tiredness. He kept letting his arms straighten to ease the pain, but it was bad for his running style and Nick was still maintaining a demanding pace.

They reached the edge of the field where a six-foot deer fence, made of pig wire, blocked their entrance to the grounds of Fountains Abbey.

'You can put those down now,' Nick said, looking at the stones, so Ian immediately dropped them as he bent over and gulped in the air.

They climbed over the flimsy fence and ran through some trees when, instantly, they came across a circular stone structure comprised of pillars and a domed roof. Ian had lost his bearings and had no idea where they were.

'This is the Temple of Fame,' Nick said. 'What do you want to be famous for?'

'Surviving,' Ian replied, jokingly.

'This next section, do flat out,' Nick ordered, as he sprinted away along a woodland track through the trees. Ian sprinted after him, keeping close on his tail. They kept this up for about 400 yards until the track opened into a small, lawned area dominated by what looked like the turret of a castle.

'This is the Octagon Tower,' Nick said.

'Hang on. I know where we are,' Ian replied. 'There's a tunnel near here. We played in it as kids. We called it Gertie's Tunnel.'

'It's called the Serpentine Tunnel,' Nick replied.

'You know more than me and I'm meant to be showing you around!' Ian grumbled, as they walked to the entrance of the tunnel, catching their breath.

'I've been studying the maps, but you have local knowledge. Both are important,' Nick reassured him.

The tunnel was made of stone with an arched ceiling

perhaps 12 feet high at its apex, so there was plenty of room to stand up in it. It was wide enough for four people to walk abreast and it was approximately 50 yards from end to end, but it was curved like a boomerang so in the middle it was completely dark. Along either side there were indentations in the stone walls, the size of large sash windows except there was no light and no glass. What they were for was a mystery.

'We used to hide in these,' Ian said, stepping up into one, 'and then we would jump out to scare the tourists.'

'Quite a prankster, were you?' Nick teased, as they trotted down to the footbridge at the top end of the lake. Ian didn't answer.

They were near the toll booth now and Nick realised they should have paid as they approached the large wrought iron gates that led back to the deer park.

'I've no money on me,' he said, 'and, anyway, I think the gates are closed.'

'Not a problem,' Ian replied and with that he vaulted a five-bar gate that led into the rear garden of the lakeside café and from there they were able to exit back into the deer park without hindrance.

'You're a rebel!' Nick taunted amicably. 'An out and out anarchist, that's what you are.'

'Mmm, let's say freedom fighter, shall we?' Ian replied thoughtfully.

'What are you fighting for?'

'Justice,' Ian retorted. 'Or fairness. After all, I am a lawyer!'

Ian was hoping for a steady pace back to the archway but Nick set off again, northwards up the steep grass embankment towards St Mary's Church. It was a climb, not a run, and Ian's knees ached as he pushed down on them.

At last, they reached the church and headed down the driveway, but then Nick took a left at the brow of the hill towards Studley Royal House and from there, back across the fields towards the village. They were not on footpaths now but crossing rough pasture, sidestepping the rougher areas to avoid turning an ankle, as they increased the pace towards the village. Nick ran even faster along Studley Lane, Ian just a few steps behind him as they turned up the drive towards the rendezvous point.

Eventually, they hit the finish line, gasping for breath and they immediately looked at each other and shook hands.

'Wow, that was amazing,' Ian said. 'I didn't know when we were going to finish.'

'That's the thing about SAS training. You never do.'

'Must be tough, mentally. How do you do it?'

'You just keep going. If you can't face the thought of what's ahead or the unknown, you just take one step at a time, or one minute at a time, or set the next rendezvous point as your only target. You just keep going or fighting until the last breath in your body. Until you win or you die trying. You just keep striving until the very end.'

Ian was still bent at the waist with his hands on his knees inhaling as much air as possible. Before he could reply, he heard the sound of feet pounding on the tarmac. He looked up and saw Rita running down the hill towards them, dressed in combat trousers, a khaki T-shirt and wearing army boots. She stopped when she saw them.

'Hello. Fancy seeing you and what's all this?' Ian asked, looking at her uniform.

'I've joined the Army Cadets,' she replied. 'I run here every day.'

'Congratulations,' Ian said as he introduced her to Nick without mentioning his military background.

Rita was sweating profusely. She said: 'hello,' to Nick, shook his hand and looked embarrassed.

'Nice to meet you Rita, but you carry on. You should never break a training run at its peak.'

Rita gave a slight nod in agreement and set off again. She was naturally fit and agile, but she also wanted to be strong. She wanted to be able to protect herself, but lying awake, in the middle of the night, she also imagined fighting Valon. A psychologist would call it a fantasy triggered by a trauma. Others might call it a premonition.

'Rita is a Kosovan refugee,' Ian said when she was out of hearing. 'I don't know if you noticed her cheek, but she had her face slashed by someone in the KLA.'

'Well, let's hope it doesn't define her,' Nick replied, as he watched her running away from them.

'What do you mean?' Ian asked.

'Well, I asked you earlier what you wanted to be famous for. Maybe I should have phrased it differently and asked what you wanted to be remembered for. What is her motivation for joining the Army Cadets?'

Ian watched her as he mulled over his response.

'What do you want to be remembered for?' he said, batting the question back to Nick.

'For defence,' Nick replied. 'For the prevention of harm. I never act in anger or seek revenge. I just protect.'

Chapter Seven

The estate agent's particulars arrived at Ian's office before Ryan Curtis had given any instructions. Holly opened the post and looked puzzled.

'Do you know anything about this?' she asked.

Ian started looking through the particulars. They were from a London agent, obviously, but not one he had heard of. The photographs were impressive. It was the show flat so every room was furnished. Fully dressed beds in the bedrooms with fitted wardrobes, pictures on the walls and even a teddy bear between the pillows. The kitchen and bathrooms were fabulous with every modern facility and the reception rooms were furnished with sofas, tables, and chairs. All for a cool six million pounds.

'No, it must be a mistake,' Ian replied, but then as he looked at the memorandum of sale he said: 'but they've got all our details correct.'

Ian was about to ring the agents to clarify the situation when Ryan Curtis entered the reception area and Holly went through to attend to him.

She thought he was unhealthily thin for a man in his early forties. He looked like he had lost weight and wore tight fitting jeans to prove it. His navy-blue polo shirt was tucked in and this ensemble was finished with a pair of expensive white trainers. He's trying too hard she thought and when she took him through to Ian, she got a whiff of smoke and curled her nose in disgust.

'So, you're the mystery buyer?' Ian said, shaking Ryan's hand. 'How did you hear about me?'

'Well, the London solicitors recommended by the estate agents wanted £20,000 for acting and I thought I would rather have a small local firm. I saw how you had renovated this place and thought you must be okay.'

The offices had been derelict when Ian bought them and he had spent six months completely refurbishing them inside and out which, given they were on a main road, had provided quite some interest for the locals.

'Crikey, I've never been chosen for the way in which I refurbished these premises before! It doesn't mean I'm a good solicitor.'

'Are you?'

'Well, I like to think so,' Ian replied.

'Right. That's sorted then.'

Ian was a little taken aback, but as it was fait accompli, he took Ryan through to the meeting room.

'So, tell me a bit about this,' Ian said, lifting the particulars off the table. 'What are your plans?'

'I work hard in my own business, don't get much time off and can't really leave the coalface to go abroad, so we thought we would buy this apartment for weekend breaks,' he paused. 'And London property is always a good investment.'

'And what is your business?'

'I'm a bookmaker. In Seacroft, but I live in Sharow,' Ryan added hastily.

'Okay, well I will contact the developer's solicitors and ask for the contract and title information and perhaps, in the meantime, you could let me have a cheque for the search fees? I normally ask for them up front. My firm's charges for acting, by the way, will be £10,000, so half the London price,' Ian said, going out on a bit of a limb.

'That's fine and I've brought you this,' Ryan replied, handing over a cheque for £600,000.

Ian looked at it and immediately realised it was for the deposit. No one had ever paid him a deposit at the outset before and it was made out to Sutherland Solicitors which was a bit presumptuous. What if I had refused to act, he thought?

'There's no need for this yet,' Ian said. 'It usually takes four weeks to get to the exchange of contracts stage.'

'Well, you might as well keep it as you will have to clear it and it might take a bit longer than normal, as you will see, it's drawn on a foreign bank.'

Ian took a second look at the cheque.

'Sevili Bank. I've never heard of it.'

'No, neither had I, but it is a gift from my wife's uncle

and that's the bank he uses. He's a Turkish Cypriot and he hasn't got any children. He has told my wife he is going to leave everything to us so he might as well start handing over his spare cash now provided we don't waste it.'

'That's kind of him,' Ian said. 'And you want me to take the search fees out of this?'

'Yes, you might as well and then I will give you a top-up cheque later.'

'Okay, well, I will just take all your contact details, please.'

'Fire away, but just before you do, is there anything that can be done to reduce the stamp duty?'

'Such as?' Ian replied, with a tone of suspicion in his voice.

'Well, what if I paid the developer something in cash?'

'You'd be arrested!' Ian said, clearly indicating his disapproval.

'It just seems a lot of money,' Ryan pleaded.

Ian looked down and started flicking through the agent's particulars again. Then he looked up.

'There's no stamp duty on teddy bears,' he said.

'I'm not with you,' Ryan replied.

'Well, you're buying the show flat. It's full of furniture and fittings. You're paying an all-in price, but it should be apportioned. You don't pay stamp duty on fittings. So, the value of the beds and other furniture should be knocked off the purchase price. In fact, the definition of a fitting is something that can removed without damaging the property, so it could include things like the fitted wardrobes.' Ian was warming to his subject. 'Leave it with me. I will have a word with the agents and see what we can do.'

'Excellent,' Ryan exclaimed, as they stood up and drew the meeting to a close. Ian saw him to the door and as he turned back into reception Holly waved him over.

'I don't like him,' she whispered.

'Why not?'

'There's something shady about him.'

'Well, I'm not going to disagree with you, as it happens. I can't really refuse to act for him now though, but we will tread carefully.'

Ian went back to his desk and rang the estate agents. A well-spoken young woman called Lucy answered the phone. Ian explained the situation to her and asked her to go back to the developer and request a schedule of fittings with a price marked against each item.

'Please stress to the developer that we are not trying to renegotiate the price. We just want to apportion a fair figure to fittings to save stamp duty,' Ian said.

'Will do,' Lucy replied.

Ian went back to his desk and picked up the telephone just as Enzo and Rita Hasani entered the office. Howard answered within two rings.

'Howard, it's Ian.'

'Hello!' Howard boomed. 'How, the devil, are you?'

'I'm well thank you Howard. How are you?'

'Stressed, as ever! What can I do for you?'

Howard was a famous London clock dealer and his showroom was located on Kensington Church Street, just a stone's throw from the apartment that Ryan Curtis intended to buy on Vicarage Gate.

Ian's little debacle in Berlin a few years ago had inspired an interest in precision timekeepers and his research had led him to Howard.

Howard's showroom was like an Aladdin's cave of the most beautiful and sought after clocks you could possibly imagine, and Ian had immediately succumbed to put his hand in his pocket and purchased a marine chronometer. Howard's knowledge and love of his stock was infectious, and Ian promised himself that if he ever had a windfall, some of the proceeds would be spent in Howard's gallery.

'I've got a client buying an apartment on Vicarage Gate,' Ian said. 'It's a new build, costing six million. I normally like to look at properties I'm acting on myself, especially if there is something exceptional about them, but there's no time in this case. As you're so near, I just wondered if you knew anything about it?'

'Of course, I do, old boy. Walk past it every day on my way to work. What do you want to know?'

'Is it all kosher? It seems like a lot of money. Is the

developer reputable? That sort of thing.'

'My dear fellow, buy that place and you can walk out of your front door into Kensington High Street or your back door into Kensington Gardens. Fabulous location,' Howard said emphatically. 'I don't know the developer but they have been on with it for months and seem to be making a good job.'

'Thanks Howard. That's helpful,' Ian replied, sounding reassured.

'When are you next coming to see me?' Howard enquired.

'I'm not sure. I've nothing planned at the moment.'

'I have a lovely Kullberg coming in. It's in original condition and perfect working order.'

'Argh, don't tell me!' Ian cried, worried the temptation would be too much. 'I'll see you soon.'

Enzo and Rita didn't have an appointment but Ian stood up and went into reception to see them.

'You exchange soon?' Enzo asked.

'Yes, I can actually,' Ian replied. 'I am just waiting for the local search to come back, but it should be okay, and, in the meantime, you could sign the contract and let me have the cheque for the deposit.'

Enzo nodded and Ian took them both into the meeting room where he went through the original conveyance with them, pointing out matters such as the restrictive covenants and he asked Enzo to sign the contract. Ian handed over copies of all the relevant documents and Enzo gave them to Rita.

'She wants to be lawyer,' Enzo said, pointing at his sister.

'Oh, really?' Ian asked. 'Which school do you go to?'

'Ripon Grammar School,' Rita replied.

'Well, you can come here for the work experience week, if you like, in July. We often have students from Ripon Grammar School.'

Rita looked down at her lap and blushed slightly.

'Yes please,' she said bashfully. Her emotions were all over the place. She was treading carefully in this new country, but she had a quiet determination to seek justice. She wanted Valon punished for what he did to her. She wanted retribution but Ian was showing her kindness and she didn't know how to respond. She didn't want to soften her heart. If anything, his kindness made her feel protective towards him which she felt was stupid, given that she was a sixteen-year-old schoolgirl and he was a grown man.

The next day Lucy called Ian back and sent over a fax comprising 12 sheets of A4 paper. It contained a closely typed list of fittings, each item individually priced, totalling £300,000 in value. The developer would agree to apportion the sale price in this way which would result in a reduction in stamp duty of £10,500.

Ian telephoned Ryan Curtis with the news. 'I've saved you enough to pay my fees,' he said triumphantly but, strangely, this elicited only a muted response, leaving Ian feeling a little deflated.

Ryan telephoned Granville who was sat at the desk in his study. He had a mug of coffee at his side and, when he heard the news, he lashed out at it, so that it flew across the desk, through the air and smashed against the wall. Coffee stained the carpet like old brown blood and pieces of crockery littered the floor.

Something for the maid to clean up he thought as he regained his composure.

'Well, you will just have to pull out,' he said. 'I was going to get you to pull out anyway, but not this soon.'

'Pull out. Why?' Ryan asked, incredulously.

'Because I want my money back. Get Sutherland to give you a client account cheque and try to get him to make it payable to Spartak Tosca.'

'But why shall I say I am pulling out?'

'That's up to you. Blame it on your wife or something. Say you will come back with fresh instructions when you find something more suitable.'

Ryan put the phone down mystified as to what was going on. He was regretting getting mixed up in all this, although the extra cash going through the betting office was useful. He rang Ian.

'I'm not going ahead,' Ryan said bluntly.

'Why not?' Ian asked, not completely surprised.

'My wife's changed her mind. She says we won't use it enough and she would rather buy a bigger house that we can live in and enjoy all year round.' Ryan smirked when he said this as his wife knew nothing about it.

'Well, if you're going to pull out, it is better to do so sooner rather than later. Less wasted costs.'

'Yes, that's what I thought. How much do I owe you? Ryan asked.

Ian weighed the file in his hand. The searches were around £200.

'Is a thousand, okay?' he asked.

'Sounds fair to me. So, can you let me have a cheque for £599,000 then? Payable to my uncle, please. We'd better give him his money back. He's called Spartak Tosca.'

'Yes, of course,' Ian replied. 'I'll post it to you tonight.'

Graham Towers was ranting at his wife as she drove back and forth between Birmingham and Coventry looking for the airport carpark.

They had booked a flight from Newcastle to Zurich as it was still too soon after the operation for Graham to drive, but the airline had cancelled the flight and, so now, they were to depart from Birmingham. This meant driving down the night before and staying at a cheap hotel to be in time for an early morning flight.

The problem was the carpark was several miles from the airport and they couldn't find it. Nor could they stop to ask anyone, as they were driving on a dual carriageway in rush hour traffic. Signage was poor, so eventually they went to the hotel and asked for directions. Then they had to drive to the carpark, and catch a shuttle bus back to the hotel. By this time, though, they were too late for a cooked dinner and had to make do with some stale sandwiches. Graham was furious. He got angry if things were outside his control. He went to bed and set the alarm for 4am to enable them to catch a 6am flight. As he tried to grab some sleep, he asked himself whether it was all worthwhile.

The next morning Graham and Kath went to check-in. They had one bag between them so Kath could wheel it along whilst Graham hobbled after her.

'It's overweight, I'm afraid,' said the girl on the check-in counter. 'You'll have to pay a surcharge.'

'What?' Graham growled. 'But we're sharing. We only have one bag between us because I've just had an operation and I can't carry anything.'

'I'm sorry sir but that makes no difference. You could check-in two smaller bags but each bag is weighed on its own merits and this one is overweight.'

'It's daylight robbery,' Graham said as he slapped the money on the counter.

They went to buy a drink and had just sat down with

a coffee when they were called through to the departure gate. Graham shot off with an awkward gait having hardly drunk anything.

On the plane, Graham was going to order a bottle of water until the air hostess said it was two pounds. He couldn't believe it. That was more than twice the going rate. Then he realised he had left his blood thinning pills in the suitcase. He huddled down in his seat fuming. He was stressed about the Roman remains. North Yorkshire County Council had requested archaeological research which would cause months of delay and he hadn't got much else on the go to occupy his men. Despite his harsh exterior he didn't like laying them off. He folded his arms tightly. Everything was going wrong.

After four hours of stubborn inactivity during which time he had hardly spoken to Kath, Graham started fidgeting as the plane prepared to land.

'What are you doing?' Kath asked, getting a little irritated by his behaviour.

'I've got cramp,' he grumbled as he bent down to scratch his right leg. 'And it's itching.'

He couldn't even get to the itchy bit because the elastic around the top of his sock was tight, but when he did, his calf felt a bit tender. This just annoyed him even more.

As soon as they disembarked, Graham set off with a fast limp towards Border Control. Kath followed dragging the bag behind her.

'Wait for me,' she shouted.

Graham turned to look at her and she could see he was struggling to catch his breath. A look of concern crossed her face as Graham clasped his chest. He fell to his knees and started coughing. Kath rushed to his side and knelt beside him. He was coughing up blood. She looked around desperately and called for help. A Border Control guard in a black uniform started saying something into a radio attached to his jacket. Graham was lying on his back now. Kath wasn't sure what to do but she took off her fleece top and folded it under his head to act as a pillow. She heard feet slapping on the airport floor. Some paramedics were running towards them.

'Help's coming,' she said. 'Hold on.'

They did some brief checks and then put Graham on a stretcher. She held his hand and had to walk quickly as they rushed him to an ambulance. He didn't say anything in the ambulance but he was watching her. She was trying to reassure him. Then he closed his eyes. He looked a bit grey. She wiped the sweat off his brow. He didn't acknowledge her and suddenly she looked up at one of the paramedics in dread. He removed her hand from her husband's forehead and kept hold of it. She feared the worse but no one said anything. They arrived at the hospital and Graham was rushed into an emergency theatre. She had to wait outside. Then a doctor came out and told her Graham had passed away.

'He was a towering figure,' she said to Ian, with an ironic smile, a week or so later as they sat in her kitchen together. 'I just can't believe he's not here anymore. I keep expecting him to walk through the door.'

She started sobbing quietly and quickly tried to wipe the tears from her eyes.

Graham had suffered a deep vein thrombosis. This caused a pulmonary embolism when the blood clot dislodged itself from his leg and travelled up into his lungs, causing a blockage. He had died of a cardiac arrest.

'I'm so very sorry,' Ian said, resting his hand on Kath's.

'You will sort everything out for me, won't you Ian?' she asked as she patted her whole face with a T-towel.

'Of course, I will, but I'm afraid I will have to do everything properly. That will mean declaring the Swiss bank account to the Inland Revenue, otherwise I could be accused of doing something illegal.'

'I understand,' Kath replied. 'I will be glad to be rid of it. It's more bother than it's worth and I wouldn't want you to get into any trouble.'

Unbeknown to Ian, he already was.

Chapter Eight

Hayden Boyes meandered into his garden with his two Rottweilers to take his usual morning constitutional. He was still wearing his pyjamas and dressing gown, and smoking a cigar as he vaguely looked at the flower borders whilst his girls went about their business.

They weren't vicious. They were just like large Labradors with docked tails, but they acted as a good deterrent, and when not in the garden, they walked either side of him like bookends, and that gave him reassurance.

His house was in the village of Leathley, built on a hillside with a walled garden and high wrought-iron gates at the entrance to the drive. The rear garden was relatively small and terraced as it had to accommodate the driveway and garage, but the front lawn was broad and gently sloping, and completely private as it was the side of the house that faced the road.

Unexpectedly, his contemplations were interrupted by the ringing of his mobile phone.

'Hello,' he said, as he lifted it from his dressing gown pocket.

'Hayden?'

'Yeah.'

'It's Freddie.'

'Oh, what do you want?' Hayden asked, with little enthusiasm.

'Our plan's going well. I got Ryan to pull out of the flat and Sutherland has paid back the money. He gave Ryan a client account cheque made payable to Spartak. We just need to build a pattern of this behaviour now as The Law Society aren't going to discipline him for a one-off event.'

Hayden mumbled something. It was hard to decipher exactly what he said, if anything. At least, that is what the GCHQ transcript noted as they were listening to every call Granville made. Criminals wised up to this eventually, but in the early days of mobile phones they had no idea.

'I want you to find another property for Ryan to buy – or not buy to be precise,' Freddie continued, laughing at his own wit. 'Make it a country estate this time – circa three million.'

'I'll see what I can do,' Hayden grunted as he pressed the button to end the call. Then he let out a long sigh so that even the dogs looked up.

Hayden had been quite keen on the idea of framing Sutherland when Granville approached him. He didn't like lawyers generally and following his father's arrest, he was spending too much time with them. He didn't like Sutherland, in particular, because he blamed him for the fact that his father would spend the rest of his life languishing in an Israeli prison and, subconsciously, because Ian's integrity highlighted his own flaws. The family had also been forced to sell their business and the proceeds were subject to claims for restitution, but he still had a bit of personal wealth and now his priority was to hang on to it.

His wife, Amy, shouted from the kitchen and lifted a cafetière skyward to indicate she had made some coffee. The dogs ran towards the house barking with excitement.

'I'm in a prison too,' Hayden muttered to himself out of self-pity.

No one would have anything to do with the family, now it was public knowledge that his father had been an officer in the SS and was guilty of the most heinous crimes. He had lost his status and his friends, the former causing the greater grief. But as Amy kept saying: 'You are not the guilty one. You are not a criminal.' He had to hold on to that. He knew he could behave a little badly sometimes, but Amy was a good woman. She had given him a daughter and she was having a positive influence on him. That was why he was planning a move to Monaco. He wanted to make a fresh start with his family and because of this he was having second thoughts about Granville's little plan. He didn't want to jeopardise their future. It was compromised enough already.

Granville sat waiting for Spartak in a replay of the

casino scene and, as before, Spartak entered via the door decorated as the Ace of Spades. Spartak paused to admire it. The whole door was covered in cream leather with the letters and symbols embossed in black leather. He made a mental note to copy it when he built his dream home.

'You always enter through the same door,' Granville said, as he stood up to greet his guest.

'Of course. The Ace of Spades is my favourite card. It is a symbol of death so I pin one to the body of anyone I kill. That way people know who to fear.' Spartak paused for dramatic effect and then continued. 'I use a lot of cards,' he shrugged, letting out a croaky chuckle at the same time.

As an opening gambit, if it was meant to unsettle, it hit the mark. Spartak was a paramilitary leader in the KLA and if questioned he could always argue his victims were casualties of war, but the fact was, they were usually casualties of turf wars which, right now, the KLA were losing.

'Come and have some champagne,' Granville said nervously. 'I have some good news for you.'

They walked from the bar to the private members area and sat down. Granville didn't even notice Spartak's new bodyguard, Polina, who had been sitting at the bar prior to either of them arriving. Wearing a grey trouser suit, slim and with bob cut brown hair, she blended into the background as intended.

'Firstly, the bank accounts,' Granville started. 'I paid your funds in Sevili Bank to the Harrogate solicitor I mentioned to you for the deposit towards an apartment in Kensington, London. My man in Harrogate then withdrew from the purchase and secured a solicitors' client account cheque in your favour which I have paid into your account with my Swiss bank. So those funds are clean, in your name and free to be used as you wish, although I stress it is a numbered account. Only three people in the bank can link your identity to the account.'

'Who are these people?' Spartak asked with a low growl.

'The chief financial officer, the chief cashier and myself. That is always the situation, for everybody. But you can access the funds simply by using the number and password and your identity will never be revealed to any foreign government or regulatory authority. That is enshrined in Swiss law.'

Spartak nodded and Granville continued.

'What I want to do is enhance this success by repeating the process, but I will need you to pay some more money into Sevili Bank.'

'Have you spent everything else?'

'Just about. You gave me one million dollars and I converted this into sterling at a rate of 1.6 which gave me about six hundred thousand pounds to play with. When I got it back, I converted this into Swiss Francs at a rate of

2.5 so you now have one and a half million in your Swiss bank account.'

Granville paused to let all this sink in and, eventually, Spartak replied.

'How much do you want?'

'Well, we have to make it worthwhile before the lawyer wises up so I thought if you could let me have another, say, half million dollars we can play the game again.'

Spartak eyed up Granville very carefully.

'It is not a game to me, Mr Frederick.'

'No, of course not. Just a figure of speech. Nevertheless, still worth doing.'

Spartak was rubbing his index finger across his mouth, searching Granville's eyes for clues.

'And you will use the same lawyer?'

'Yes.'

'Why?'

Granville was taken off guard and spluttered his reply.

'Well, it has worked once and my man on the ground is building up a track record with the lawyer.' He paused. 'You see the first property fell through so he has a reason to go back to try again with a second purchase. That's the picture we're painting for the lawyer. It makes sense.'

There was a slight nervousness in Granville's voice and Spartak was watching his every move. At last, he nodded in agreement.

'And there is more to tell me?'

'Yes, the second thing. Proceeds from the sale of cigarettes in the UK are being laundered through a betting shop in Leeds and the net amount is being accumulated in a UK high street bank for you. Just small amounts so far, but I've set up a limited company in the UK to receive the monies for security services rendered to the bookmaker, and this company is wholly owned by another company which I've registered in the Cayman Islands. That company is owned by a trust to be registered in Switzerland once I have your instructions regarding the ultimate beneficiaries.'

Granville paused for breath and smiled but Spartak didn't look impressed.

'Granit tells me we get just six thousand out of every ten?'

'Yes, that's correct but the six thousand looks legitimate.'

'I might as well just pay the tax,' Spartak protested.

Granville shuffled his position and looked uncomfortable. He wasn't sure what to say. Spartak changed tack.

'Why are we pulling out of these properties? I thought I was going to buy them.'

'Not with dirty money,' Granville shot back. 'We clean the money first and then buy something with it. We have to accumulate enough clean money first otherwise the authorities might ask questions.'

Spartak understood this but he was testing the water. He hadn't made his money by trusting people and he looked at Granville with a deep suspicion.

'There's no need for me to have a security business to charge this bookmaker for fake services. I should just own the betting shop and launder the money through it myself.'

'Er, you could do that,' Granville replied, trying to think on his feet, 'but the bookmaker might not want to sell.'

Spartak laughed out loud and shook his head at Granville as though he was completely naïve.

'Then Granit will persuade him,' he said.

Ryan Curtis was quicker off the mark this time and made an appointment to see Ian before the estate agent sent through any particulars.

Hayden had found an appropriate property, but he had decided that this would mark the end of his involvement. Unfortunately, he omitted to tell anyone else and exiting a partnership was not always as easy as joining one.

Hayden was also getting careless. The property was not being marketed through the normal channels. In fact, it wasn't even on the market yet. He had been given the nod by the estate agent that hoped to get the business and so, to tie things up quickly, he agreed to meet Ryan with the details. There was the added complexity that the owner was a reluctant seller.

'It's three million,' Ryan said loudly, intending Holly to hear, as he swaggered towards the meeting room with Ian. 'It's got one hundred acres and a massive house, but it needs everything doing to it. It's off market, but they've accepted my offer so long as we act quickly.'

'What will you do with a hundred acres?' Ian asked.

'Let it out probably. It's let out at the moment so we can just allow the same farmer carry on, but the house will make an interesting project for Cindy and it will be a great place for the kids to grow up.'

'Cindy being your wife, I take it?'

'Yes.'

'I'll need to go and see it,' Ian said, 'especially if there are no sales particulars.'

'Fine, and here's a little something from uncle,' Ryan said, sliding a cheque across the table.

Ian looked at it. £300,000, drawn on Sevili Bank.

'Same scenario as before?' he asked.

'Yes, generous uncle.'

'Okay, I will take the search fees out of this, but I will still have to charge you £10,000 for my fees because with all the land and, presumably, a farm business tenancy, I can see there will be a lot of work involved.'

'No problem. Just let me know when you next want to see me, but remember it's off market so we need to show we are moving quickly.'

'I'll get on to it straight away but just clarify this. Who is my client? You, your wife or both of you?'

'Me,' Ryan replied, looking surprised.

'But if your wife's uncle is supplying the purchase monies, won't he want to see her name on the title deeds?'

Ryan looked stumped.

'Oh yes, of course. I see what you mean now. Joint names please.'

'Fine, I will arrange a viewing as soon as I can.'

As soon as he was out of the door Ian, Ed and Holly all looked at each other.

'I don't like it,' said Ed. 'Something is not right.'

'I agree with you,' Ian replied, 'but I can't put my finger on it.'

'I don't like HIM,' Holly chipped in. 'He's a slime ball.'

'Well, I will go and see the property and just take one step at a time, but one thing's for certain.'

'What?' Holly and Ed chimed in unison.

'We need to meet his wife.'

The property was just a few miles outside Ripon and it was called Abbot's Park. It was owned by a charity and used as a home for children with Down's syndrome.

Ian pulled up to the entrance gates and drove up the long drive towards the house. The drive was bordered by fields grazed by sheep and the house was a grey stone, sprawling monstrosity with numerous outbuildings all constructed in the same vernacular.

Signage guided Ian into a carpark but, before he could get his bearings, a woman appeared from a back door accompanied by, Ian assumed given his dog-collar, a member of the clergy.

'Hello,' Ian said walking up to her. 'I'm Ian Sutherland from Sutherland Solicitors. I'm here to see Anne Shaw.'

'I'm Anne Shaw,' the woman replied icily.

She had light grey, curly hair and was middle-aged; she wore no make-up and was slightly over-weight.

'Oh, that's good. Well, I wanted a quick look around if that's okay with you?'

'Do I have any choice?' Again, the sharpness in her voice was not difficult to detect.

'I don't need to go inside,' Ian reassured her. 'I just need a walk around outside.'

'What for?' She was hostile now and Ian was wondering how he had managed to get off on the wrong foot so quickly.

'Well, I want to check the boundaries and make sure they accord with the Land Registry plan. Check that there have been no encroachments or incorporations of land outside the plan. Then I want to check rights of way such as footpaths and wayleaves for telephone and electricity lines – that sort of thing.'

'Well, I haven't time to show you around! We have a

hundred acres!'

Before Ian could say anything, the clergyman interjected.

'Perhaps I could show Mr Sutherland around Anne? I'm Harold Steadman, by the way, how do you do?'

'How do you do?' Ian replied, shaking his hand.

Anne was a little taken aback and softened, but only slightly.

'Well, if you don't mind, Harold?'

'No trouble at all,' he replied, giving her a kindly smile.

'This way please,' Harold said, placing a guiding arm gently on Ian's shoulder.

Harold must have been close to retirement age. He wore charcoal grey trousers and a lighter grey herringbone tweed jacket with black, derby style shoes. He was of average size and build with grey hair and he was softly spoken but, nevertheless, his voice commanded authority.

They walked up the remaining part of the drive together towards the front entrance.

'Don't worry about Anne's abruptness. She's feeling a little sensitive at the moment,' Harold said, trying to repair the damage.

'Why is that?' Ian asked.

There was a game of football going on in an adjacent field and the sound of children laughing rang in their ears. It looked somewhat chaotic but they were clearly enjoying themselves.

'Well, you see, the charity is a forced seller. The roof is leaking to such an extent that we have had to abandon the top floor and there are essential electricity repairs which are required to meet the latest health and safety regulations. The charity needs £300,000 just to bring the property up to spec and they simply haven't got it. So the idea is to sell and buy something smaller, but Anne's taken it very badly because the children are happy here.'

'I see,' Ian replied, as they reached the end of the drive and looked over the fields at the rear of the property.

They were large and arable, while the fields to the front were laid down to pasture, but between the two was a thick hedge on the left-hand side of the house. On the right-hand side was the rear garden of the house behind which was a small wood.

Suddenly, a fox trotted out of the wood no more than 20 yards in front of them. It gave them a cursory glance and then continued to the hedge where it stopped to sniff something. It was in fine summer fettle and despite being aware of their presence made no attempt to depart.

'Wow! look at that,' Ian said, pointing towards the fox.

'That's a co-incidence. I've just given the children a talk about a fox,' Harold said, chuckling softly. 'They like animal stories.'

'What did you say?' Ian asked with genuine interest.

'Do you really want to know?'

'Yes.'

'Well, it's apocryphal, but I told them a story that in Biblical times a Man of God goes into the desert to spend time thinking and he meets a shepherd. The shepherd invites him to dine with him and the Man of God gladly accepts. When they finish their meal, the shepherd gets a bowl of milk and puts it outside his tent on a small rocky outcrop. 'What are you doing?' asks the Man of God. 'I am giving God his share,' the shepherd replies. The Man of God laughs at him. 'God doesn't drink the milk,' he said, but the shepherd insists that he does, so the Man of God suggests they sit up all night and watch to see what happens. In the dead of night, a desert fox creeps into the camp and laps up the milk. 'You see,' scoffs the Man of God, 'it's nothing to do with God.' The shepherd goes to bed disheartened and at daybreak the Man of God goes on his way. In an instant, he is dazzled by a bright light and a voice from heaven says: 'the shepherd gave the milk to me and I chose to share it with the fox.'

Ian thought about it for a while.

'So, what's the moral of the story?' he asked.

'Well, on one level, it speaks to the arrogance of man. We think we know best when, actually, we understand very little but, for the children, the point I wanted to make is that God cares for all his creation. The shepherd paid homage to God and when God thought of the fox he thought of the shepherd.'

'Foxes seem to keep coming up in my life,' Ian said a

little glumly. 'I don't know if it's a good or a bad omen.'

'Tell me,' Harold said, almost whispering.

Ian looked into Harold's eyes and wanted to explain everything. He gushed out his story.

'You may have read about this in the local paper, but a few years ago, a man called Frederick Granville ran me over. He tried to kill me. His father was called Manfred Fuchs and he had been an officer in the SS. Fuchs is German for fox and I acted for an ex-marine who had shot him during the war. Granville was the heir apparent to Granville's Bank and, I suppose, I exposed the family for what they were. They had been lending money to the Nazis. They lost everything and Frederick Granville ended up in prison.' Ian paused and took a deep breath.

'More recently, I have acted for a builder who wanted to stop the local hunt crossing his land and now we've just seen this fox,' Ian said, pointing towards the hedge.

Harold gave Ian a kindly smile.

'I wouldn't think of foxes as a good or bad omen,' he said, 'but think of them as a warning. If you see a fox, be alert.'

Chapter Nine

Ryan stuck out his tongue and looked in the mirror. A large cyst, the size of a garden pea, protruded from its tip. It wasn't painful, but he was worried so he had spoken to his GP who had referred him to a specialist at the Leeds University dental school. He hadn't told Cindy.

'Just sign this will you love?' he said, placing the contract for the purchase of Abbot's Park in front of her on the kitchen table.

'What is it?'

'Just an investment. I'm doing it in joint names so I can make you some money,' he reassured her.

'Oh, lovely,' she replied, holding the pen with her fingers straight owing to the length of her false nails. She lifted her face and smiled at him as she passed back the document. Ryan put it in an envelope and smiled back at her sheepishly.

'Can you post it as well? I'm going to the dentist.'

'Of course,' she replied.

Cindy looked at the address as Ryan rushed out of the door. She was going to have her hair done in Harrogate and her hairdresser was on Station Parade, quite near Ian's office. I might as well hand deliver it, she thought.

She parked her Mercedes right outside the hairdressers and trotted in her heels across the busy junction where Victoria Avenue intersected Station Parade.

'Just dropping this off,' she said, as she handed the envelope to Holly.

Ian jumped up from his seat as she turned to go.

'Excuse me. Are you Mrs Curtis, by any chance?'

'Yes,' she replied.

Ian left his desk and came towards her.

'Hello, I'm Ian Sutherland. I've been wanting to meet you.'

Cindy looked completely blank.

'You've brought the contract back for me, have you?'

'Yes,' she answered, a little distractedly.

'Would you like to come through and have a chat about it?'

'I'm going to get my hair done,' she said, checking her watch.

'I won't keep you long,' Ian persisted.

Cindy looked at her watch again.

'You've got five minutes,' she said firmly.

Ian showed her through to the meeting room.

'I just wanted to check you were happy with the purchase and wondered if you had any questions?'

'I don't know anything about it,' she snapped.

'But you have signed the contract?'

'Yes, but I leave all that sort of thing to Ryan.'

'And is your uncle happy with everything?'

'Uncle? I haven't got an uncle.'

'But the purchase price is being provided by your uncle? In Cyprus?'

'Look, I'm sorry,' she said, 'but I am going to get my hair done. If you have any questions ask Ryan.'

She swept out of the door leaving Ian and Holly watching her vanish down the road. Ian looked dumbfounded.

'What's up?' Holly asked.

Ian told her everything.

'It's a mucocele,' the dentist said, after prodding around in Ryan's mouth.

'What's that?' Ryan asked, trying to formulate the words so that they were comprehensible, even though he still had a dental mirror and probe stretching the sides of his mouth.

'You seem to have cauterised a salivary gland causing an accumulation of fluid. Tell me, are you aware of burning your tongue recently?'

'No.'

'When did you first notice it?'

'Sunday evening. When I went to bed.'

'And what did you have to eat on Saturday evening?'

'Pizza.'

'Did you eat it as soon as it came out of the oven?'

'Erm, yes.'

'And did you, by any chance, test to see how hot it was with the end of your tongue?'

'Erm, yes, yes, I think I did,' Ryan replied excitedly.

'Well, there's your answer. You've sealed a salivary gland on the end of your tongue.'

'So, what do we do?' Ryan asked anxiously.

'Nothing to start with. It may go away on its own but if not, we may have to freeze it. We have a range of options, but let's leave it for a week or two and see what happens.'

'So, it's not serious?'

'Not in this case, but less of the lizard like tongue action in future please!' the dentist said light-heartedly to reduce the tension.

Ryan left the dental school and sat down on the retaining wall of a flowerbed just outside to catch his breath. He debated about having a cigarette. He wanted one but he had been worried about his tongue and it seemed churlish to tempt fate just after he had received a reprieve. He was jolted from this reverie by the ringing of his phone.

'Ryan?'

'Yes.'

'It's Hayden. I've got Granville's henchmen with me and we are just on our way to see you.' Hayden was sat in the back of the car and hoped Granit and Valon would not understand the subtleties of his language or his intonation.

'I'm at the dentists.'

'Where's that? We have just come through Bramhope and we were going to take the ring road to Seacroft.'

'What's it about?'

'A business proposition. Granville was insistent that we meet you. He wants me to translate the details.'

'Okay, well carry straight on through Headingley and then turn right down Clarendon Road. At the bottom of Clarendon Road, turn left down Mount Preston Street and I will meet you outside Charlie Mo Hall. We can go for a coffee on Red Route.'

When built, Red Route was the longest corridor in Europe, forming a spine of concrete and glass linking the brutalist concrete buildings that made up the university campus. Supported by concrete pillars where it linked the buildings, it mainly ran at third floor level depending on the contour of the ground beneath.

'So, what's the business proposition this time?' Ryan asked, with one exhaled breath, once they had all sat down with their coffees.

'Granville's a banker,' Hayden explained. 'He looks after the investments of a Kosovan paramilitary leader called Spartak. Granit and Valon really work for him.' Hayden paused whilst Ryan's eyes flicked back and forth.

'And?'

'Spartak wants to buy your business.'

'It's not for sale,' Ryan replied, without needing time to think about it.

'You haven't heard the offer yet.'

'Go on then.'

'£300,000. You've already got the money which is lodged with that solicitor. You sign over the business and then you pull out of the purchase of Abbot's Park and the money is yours to do what you want with.'

'No,' Ryan said emphatically.

'I think you should take some time to consider,' Hayden replied, with a note of caution in his voice.

'I don't need to. What am I meant to live off when the money runs out?' Ryan turned towards Granit and Valon. 'Tell this Spartak that the answer is no.'

Granit was sat, leaning forwards, his arms resting on his thighs with his hands holding the coffee cup between his legs. He had been staring at the floor, but now looked up simply by lifting his head a few inches.

'I think you should reconsider,' he said, in his deep guttural accent.

Ryan's eyes darted again from one person to another.

'No. The answer's no,' he confirmed nervously as he stood up to leave.

Hayden jumped up and quickly followed with Granit and Valon trailing behind him. He came up beside Ryan as they reached a concrete bridge, with open sides at chest height, linking two buildings. Hayden said something like: 'Look, I don't think these are people you can mess with,' when suddenly, Granit tapped his hand on Ryan's shoulder.

'Nice view,' he said, turning Ryan towards the opening.

Ryan looked over the side of the bridge. There was not much of a view. Just more buildings with some green landscaping and a paved square some 25 to 30 feet below. He turned his head slightly to give them a puzzled look just as Granit and Valon gripped him with a hand on each shoulder and with their other hands on the back of his jeans. With one swift move they threw him head first over the edge. Two seconds later he hit the ground.

'What are you doing?' Hayden screamed in utter panic.

'Now, maybe he reconsiders,' Granit grunted as he and his brother walked calmly away from the scene.

Hayden rushed to the end of the bridge and ran down the steps to where Ryan lay unconscious with a pool of dark crimson blood seeping from his head. He pulled his mobile phone from his pocket and rang 999.

An ambulance seemed to arrive almost immediately. Hayden was pacing around in panic and couldn't face looking at Ryan. A small crowd of passers-by had gathered around, but no one dared to do anything. However, it was clear from the chatter that Ryan was still alive.

Hayden identified himself to the paramedics and, at their suggestion, joined them in the ambulance. In a completely distracted manner, he answered some basic questions. He gave Ryan's name and address and the name of his wife, but he said he didn't see what happened.

They didn't believe him and made sure they had a note of his name and address.

When they arrived at the hospital, Ryan was rushed into an operating theatre. There was nothing Hayden could do so he got a taxi home.

'Are you fucking mad?' Hayden screamed at Granville after he had relayed the events to him.

Granville held the phone away from his ear until Hayden had calmed down.

'Granit and Valon work for Spartak. I don't control them,' he replied.

'Well, I'm out of it. Finished. I want nothing more to do with you or your mad friends. Don't ever contact me again,' he said, as he squashed the red button on his phone.

Hayden wandered out into his garden and sat on a teak bench with his head in his hands. The dogs came over and nuzzled him, demanding attention. They could tell there was something wrong. So could Amy when she arrived home.

'What is it, babe?' she asked, sitting down beside him on the bench.

He told her what had happened to Ryan, trembling as he did so. She put an arm around his hunched shoulders.

'Look, babe. Your father was a bad man, but you're not. I understand you love him but he did bad things. You didn't! You don't have to carry this burden for him. You can't undo what he did, but you can help make things better. You're confusing loyalty with right and wrong. You can still love him, but you don't have to support this mad Granville scheme for revenge,' she said, her voice rising with stress.

'I'm not. I've told him I don't want anything more to do with it,' Hayden replied in an equally high-pitched tone.

'Well, I think you ought to go and see this solicitor and warn him. That is something you can do to lessen the damage, before he gets thrown off a bridge as well!'

'I will. I will. I will go tomorrow morning.'

Amy stood up to go back into the house, but stopped and turned to face Hayden after she had only taken a few paces.

'We're not in any danger, are we?' she asked anxiously.

'No, of course not,' Hayden replied, trying to reassure her. He let his head sink towards his knees and shook it in despair. His arms and legs were shaking. He hoped he had put her mind at rest, but he was scared.

The next morning Hayden watched Holly open the office from his parked car. He then saw Ed arrive, followed shortly by Ian. He jumped out of the car, dashed across the road, and burst into reception.

'Can I see Ian Sutherland please? It's urgent,' he said to Holly without any preliminary pleasantries.

Ian had seen him enter and before Holly could reply, he came over.

'What do you want?' Ian asked with some hostility as he immediately recognised Hayden and remembered that the last time they had spoken, Hayden had been verbally abusive.

'I'm sorry but I must speak to you. There are things you need to know.'

Ian could see the panic in Hayden's eyes and his flushed face made it obvious that this was something serious.

'Go ahead,' Ian replied, without inviting Hayden into the meeting room. Whatever this was about, he wanted Ed and Holly to be witnesses. This left Hayden feeling a little awkward but he carried on.

'Ryan Curtis. You know Ryan Curtis? He's been thrown off a bridge on Red Route. At Leeds university.' He nodded questioningly to check Ian understood. 'His face is smashed to pieces. His jaw and cheek bones are broken in over 20 places and the doctors say when he comes out of hospital, he will look completely different. His face will be smaller and rounder. He can only take in fluids because his jaw is all wired up and that's just the facial injuries.'

Hayden was rushing to get the words out and Ian watched him carefully.

'Why are you telling me this and what's your involvement?' Ian asked calmly.

'I'm sorry, but you're being set up. Frederick Granville wants revenge and Ryan is taking his instructions from Granville. I found Ryan for Granville. I'm sorry; I feel terrible now.'

Hayden sank into one of the chairs in reception and lent forward with his arms on his thighs and his head almost between his knees.

'Do you want some water?' Holly asked.

'Yes, good idea,' Ian said, leaning against the edge of Holly's desk. 'Give him some water.'

Holly handed him a glass of tap water.

'Thanks,' Hayden said, taking a long gulp.

'Now, tell me, just how does Granville intend to set me up?' Ian asked. There was no sympathy in his voice. Mentally, Ian was in court conducting a cross-examination.

'Granville wants revenge for what you did to him. He lives in northern Cyprus now and provides banking facilities, mostly for criminals! He's acting for a Kosovan paramilitary leader called Spartak whose got two thugs over here called Granit and Valon,' Hayden paused and drank some more water.

'Granville asked me to find a stooge over here that would launder money for him, Spartak, I mean. We needed a cash generative business that could process cash without drawing attention from the authorities – so I found Ryan. Then Spartak decided he wanted to buy the business and when Ryan refused Granit and Valon threw him off the bridge!'

'I don't see how this involves me?' Ian said as Ed started shuffling in his seat. He was about to say something but Hayden continued.

'Granville's idea is that Ryan keeps giving you money to buy things and then pulls out of the transaction so you return the money clean. When he has built up a track record of this, Granville is going to report you to the Law Society for money laundering. He wants you struck off the solicitors' roll and your reputation ruined.' Hayden's voice softened and then he continued: 'He wants you to go to prison.'

Ian sat silently for a few moments and looked at Ed who was looking at Ian. Holly was sat behind Ian but she slid her chair to the side so all three of them could share a worried look.

'Well, thank you for telling me,' Ian replied in a matter-of-fact sort of way. 'Does Spartak know about Granville's little scheme?'

'I don't think so.'

'And Ryan?'

'I don't think he knows the details, but he knows Granville is up to something. I think he regrets getting involved with him. Well, he will now!' Hayden exclaimed as he slumped back in the chair and let out a sigh of relief.

'So, where does all this leave you?' Ian asked.

'I'm out of it. I've told Granville. We're moving to

Monaco.'

'And you think your friends will accept your resignation?'

'I hope so. I've not had any involvement with Spartak, just Granville. I'm going to move and keep a low profile. I've got a wife and daughter to think about.'

'Well, I'm grateful for the warning,' Ian said, as he straightened up and held out his hand. 'I'd get to Monaco as soon as I could if I was you.'

'Yes, I will. Thank you and, erm, I'm sorry.'

'Okay,' Ian replied.

Hayden scuttled out the office and Ian closed the door behind him.

'I knew it was a money laundering thing,' Ed said, jumping up, as soon as Ian had closed the door.

'Are we in trouble?' Holly asked anxiously.

'I hope not,' Ian replied. 'We are going to have to think about everything very carefully.'

'But what are we going to do?' she appealed, her eyes moistening.

'There is one thing we could do,' Ian said, picking up the contract dropped off by Cindy and waving it in front of them.

'What?' they both chimed in unison.

'We could exchange.'

Chapter Ten

The next morning Rita entered the offices of Sutherland Solicitors to see Ian, Ed and Holly all huddled around a table in reception, obviously deep in conversation. She stood in silence, unsure what to say, until Ian jumped up and welcomed her.

'Hello, Rita. Welcome to Sutherland Solicitors! We are just having our morning meeting, so you can come and join us if you like? Here, have a seat,' Ian said, pulling up another chair.

'Is that wise?' Ed asked.

'Rita is from Kosovo and, as Granville is in cahoots with a Kosovan paramilitary leader, she may have something useful to add – you never know. Have you ever heard of someone called Spartak?' Ian asked her

Rita shook her head.

'Yes, bit of a longshot,' Ian sighed. 'Anyway, we are just discussing the pros and cons of exchanging contracts on a property called Abbot's Park.'

'I go?'

'No, you can stay if you like.'

'I don't see how you can exchange contracts. You

haven't got the clients' authority to do so,' Ed interjected, to bring the conversation back to business.

'Both Mr and Mrs Curtis have signed the contract,' Ian replied. 'There is no proof that we haven't got their authority and we've got their deposit.'

'But you know you would normally get confirmation just before you exchanged.'

'Yes, but are they likely to complain? Ryan is in no fit state to do anything and Mrs Curtis hasn't got a clue what's going on?'

'All the more reason not to exchange!' Ed stressed.

'Yes Ed, I would agree with you in normal circumstances, but these aren't normal circumstances. Let's analyse the facts, shall we? If we don't exchange contracts, presumably, Granville will ask for his money back either via Ryan Curtis or, if he's not up to it, his wife. We will then have assisted him in laundering money and he will report me to the authorities. I may be able to explain myself out of trouble but there will be a pattern. I have done it before, albeit inadvertently, with the London flat.

If we do exchange contracts, I'm not guilty of money laundering or, if I am, it is much less obviously so. I think the Law Society would consider it an accident rather than a scheme of arrangement.'

'I don't understand,' Holly said quickly, to get a word in edgeways. 'Why isn't it money laundering if we buy the house?'

'I think it is a matter of presumption,' Ed replied. 'There has been a red flag warning to solicitors from the Law Society about clients giving instructions, paying over money, and then pulling out of the transaction and asking for the money to be returned. So, they would argue we should have been alert to the situation, especially as Ryan has done it before. If we exchange, on the other hand, we may be technically assisting him launder money by facilitating an investment, but how were we to know? He will not have acted any differently from a normal client.'

'Nicely put,' Ian said.

There was a pause whilst they all processed the idea and then Ed started again.

'I think you're forgetting something though. If we exchange contracts we will have to complete.'

'Or not,' Ian replied.

Ed's eyes widened. 'But if you don't complete Granville will lose his deposit!'

'Exactly. That's what I want. We can't be done for money laundering if the client loses the money!'

Ed slumped back into his chair whilst Holly and Rita just looked at each other in dismay. Ed lent forward.

'Are you saying you will exchange contracts knowing that Granville cannot complete causing him to lose his deposit? It's too risky.'

'What I'm saying is this. We exchange contracts

with a standard completion date 20 working days later. I doubt Granville will have the funds to complete because he isn't expecting to pay over the balance. If the seller then rescinds the contract, they can keep the deposit. They don't want to sell anyway and the deposit will go a long way towards paying for the essential repairs to the property. If Granville does complete, the charity is no worse off than they expected.'

'And what if Granville sets Granit and Valon on to you?'

'Excuse me?' Rita interrupted, looking alarmed.

'Oh, this Granville chap has a couple of Kosovan thugs working for him called Granit and Valon. You don't know them by any chance?' Ian asked expecting a negative answer.

'Yes,' Rita replied. 'They are bad. Very bad. Valon did this to me,' she said, pointing to the scar on her cheek.

Everyone was silent and looked at her as the severity of the situation sank in. Eventually, Ian broke the tension.

'Well, they can't harm Ryan. They've already done that so we are not putting him at any risk and I've dealt with Granville before. By exchanging contracts, we will smoke him out, so to speak, and hopefully deal with him once and for all.'

'A hundred percent. I would do it,' Holly said.

'I wouldn't. There are too many unknown risks,' Ed countered.

Rita just said: 'Do it,' which impressed Ian because he was surprised she had understood the legal argument.

'I'm going to sleep on it and then decide,' Ian replied. 'I realise it's a risk, but it's a calculated one.'

However, one thing had not been weighed in Ian's calculations – the fact that Granville was using Spartak's money.

The shocks just kept on coming. Ian had written to the Inland Revenue regarding the death of Graham Towers and revealed the existence of the Swiss bank account but said, at this stage, he had no further details. He asked for guidance as to how he should proceed and was expecting a helpful reply, but instead, the Inland Revenue simply wrote to him saying they had frozen the estate until the amount in the Swiss bank account was declared. Nothing could be done until this was sorted. No money could be accessed, so Ian couldn't even pay the undertaker.

Ian broke the news to Kath who luckily had some cash available for her own essentials and she said she would pay the undertaker herself, to save him waiting.

'There's nothing for it,' Ian said. 'I'm just going to have to go to Zurich and access the bank account details personally,' he paused. 'Unless, of course, you would rather go?'

'Oh, no. I don't want to go,' Kath replied emphatically. 'I would much rather you dealt with it, then, at least, I know it will all be dealt with properly.'

'Okay, and you know the account number and password?'

'I know where they are written down,' she confirmed.

'Great, and what's the name of the bank?'

'Granville's,' she replied.

There was complete silence but, for Ian, it was as though a bomb had just exploded and he was deafened by shell shock.

'Is everything okay?' Kath asked.

'Fine. I'll handle it,' Ian mumbled as he put the phone down.

Something deep down told Ian he had to deal with this man. He would go to Zurich with the account number and password, and obtain details of the sums involved for the Inland Revenue because the bank wouldn't disclose anything over the telephone, or in writing. But there was more to it than this. Something was gnawing at his gut. Frederick Granville kept appearing in his life and he felt there was an element of evil at play. This needed to be excised and without really understanding how it would help, Ian exchanged contracts on Abbot's Park. He wasn't sure why, but he believed it was the right thing to do.

Ian drove at a crawl up the driveway to Abbot's Park, watching the children playing on the games field as he did so. As the E-type pulled into the carpark, Anne Shaw observed his approach, her eyes firing daggers at him. She hated everything he represented. The wealthy lawyer with the fancy suits and car. Probably, a right-wing, capitalist pig, mercilessly pursuing profit at everyone else's expense.

'Come to gloat, have you?' she asked, as Ian got out of the car.

'I'm sorry?' Ian replied.

'Come to check we're packing up? Come to make sure everything is ready so your client can have a nice big house to live in?'

'Not at all,' Ian said, looking embarrassed.

Luckily, Harold appeared from the kitchen, probably attracted by Anne's shouting.

'I'll look after Mr Sutherland,' he said to Anne.

He put an arm around Ian's shoulder and guided him towards the playing fields.

'How can we help you?' he asked, as they wandered in the direction of the children.

'What's up with her?' Ian said, glancing back over his shoulder.

'Oh, pay no attention to Anne. I think she is finding the prospect of leaving Abbot's Park very stressful.'

'Well, that's what I want to talk to you about. I don't think that will be necessary.'

Harold stopped in his tracks. 'I don't follow,' he said.

They watched the children for a moment. It was sports day and someone attracted their attention by shouting 'go.' About eight teenagers were racing down the track. It looked like the 100 metres. Arms, and legs were flaying about all over the place which caused one of the children to trip and hit the ground. Without exception, the others stopped and helped the casualty to his feet, fussing to check he was all right.

'You look surprised?' Harold suggested as Ian watched in wonder.

'Erm, yes,' Ian replied. 'Funny how they all stopped. In fact, to be honest, I didn't realise you would have a sports day.'

'We try to make things as normal as possible, but they lack the killer instinct, you see. Generally, they have a very caring nature.'

Ian felt a knot in the base of his stomach. 'But you've got to have people with a killer instinct?' he implored.

'Of course. It's all part of life's great tapestry. Look at soldier ants. They fight off predators threatening the colony. Everything is mirrored in nature,' Harold replied, with a gentle sigh of acceptance. 'Anyway, you were saying something about us not having to leave?'

'Yes, but this conversation has to remain confidential,' Ian replied. 'I shouldn't really be speaking to you at all.'

'Well, you obviously feel it is the right thing to do, so please continue and, of course, the conversation will remain privileged.'

'Okay,' Ian said, taking a deep breath. 'I've just found

out that the buyer of Abbot's Park, Ryan Curtis, is a stooge for a banker living in northern Cyprus called Frederick Granville. Can you remember? I told you about him. He's the man that ran me over.'

'Oh, yes, of course. He sounded a nasty piece of work.'

'Well, apparently, he has a plot to get me struck off the Solicitors' Roll for money laundering. It works like this. Ryan Curtis instructs me to buy a property, gives me a deposit with dirty money and then pulls out. I then must repay him and the money, coming from my solicitor's client account, is clean.'

'I see. And how do you know all this?'

'Oh, it gets even more complex, but Ryan Curtis was thrown off a bridge by some Kosovan thugs and the man acting as a go-between for Granville panicked and told me everything.'

'Ian, this all sounds very strange and dangerous to me. Don't you think you should tell the police?' Harold cautioned.

'Well, I assume they will be questioning Ryan Curtis about being thrown off the bridge. He survived, by the way, but I can't tell them about this money laundering scheme. We couldn't prove anyone has done anything wrong yet. Anyway, I have my own plan.'

'Yes, explain that to me. It seems to involve us not moving?'

'Yes. So, I exchanged contracts, as you know. That

means I haven't done anything wrong - in the eyes of the Law Society. So, I won't be done for money laundering,' Ian said, rushing out the information.

'I'm trying to follow you, Ian,' Harold said gently, 'but I still don't see why we don't have to move out.'

'Because Granville won't be able to complete. I'm pretty sure he won't be able to pay the balance of the purchase price because it was never his intention to do so. I don't think he will have the money.'

'But where does that leave us?' Harold asked, still having no idea of the end game.

'It leaves you here! Under the Law Society's Standard Conditions of Sale, if Granville doesn't complete on time, your solicitor can serve a notice to complete which gives Granville another ten working days to come up with the money. If he doesn't, you can rescind the contract and keep the deposit.'

'Keep the deposit?'

'Yes.'

'You mean we can just keep the £300,000?'

'Yes.'

'And we still own the property?'

'Yes.'

Harold stared over the playing fields as he let the information sink in.

'So, you are telling me we can keep the £300,000, spend it on renovations, if we wish, and stay here?'

'Yes. Provided, Granville doesn't complete.'

Harold started nodding repeatedly as he realised the implications. He looked at the children and said: 'When God thought of them, he thought of you.'

Ian was taken aback. 'No,' he replied, looking embarrassed. 'I'm just saving my own skin.'

Harold smiled kindly at him. 'No, Ian. God knows your character and when he thought of them, he thought of you.' He paused for a moment and then continued: 'And there's no greater privilege.'

Ryan Curtis sat at his kitchen table with Cindy sat next to him. In his left hand he nestled a glass of water which he was drinking with the aid of a straw, as his jaw was wired together. His right hand protruded from a plaster of Paris and Cindy was gently holding it in her hand.

'You were lucky you weren't more badly injured,' she said, trying to encourage him.

Ryan gave a tiny, ironic smile. His right arm had taken the brunt of the fall to start with and broken under the strain. A split second later, his face had absorbed the rest of the impact. He couldn't bear to see himself in the mirror. He would never look the same again.

They were both staring at a letter from Ian informing them that he had exchanged contracts with a completion date 20 working days later. One of those days had already passed.

Ryan used his left hand to push a notepad under his right hand and then wrote: *you need to ring Granville*. He then slid the notepad across to Cindy.

Reluctantly, because no one else could, Cindy did so and read Granville the contents of the letter.

'What?' Granville shouted in a state of apoplexy. 'Put Ryan on.'

Now it was Cindy's turn. She hurled a tirade of abuse at Granville which surprised even him. She said things like: 'He's lucky to be alive. He can't even speak,' and 'no thanks to you.' In fact, the insults came so quickly, one after another, it was hard for Granville to compute them at the time or remember them afterwards. This made him even more angry because he wasn't used to people shouting at him.

'He will not beat me,' he screamed at one point, referring to Ian.

'Have you no mercy man?' Cindy responded, not really understanding what Granville meant.

'Revenge knows no mercy,' he snarled as he slammed down the phone.

He was fuming with anger. He picked a paperweight up from his desk and threw it against the wall leaving a circular break in the plasterboard. He cleared his desk with one sweep of his arm and kicked the wastepaper basket into the corner.

Breathless, he slumped back into his chair, red-faced

and sweating. He picked up the telephone and rang Granit.

'That solicitor, Ian Sutherland,' he said. 'Kill him.'

Chapter Eleven

Nick Rowe entered Fortnum & Mason via the Piccadilly entrance and made for the marmalade and jam section on the ground floor, as instructed. Simon Black handed him a jar of 'The Monarch.'

'This is the one you should buy. It has a tangy citrus flavour that is masked by sweeter marmalades.'

Nick Rowe accepted the jar nonchalantly but got straight down to business.

'You've seen the GCHQ transcript?'

'Keep your voice down,' Black replied, in a fierce whisper. 'I brought you here because the background noise from the tourists will make it difficult to decipher our conversation, but we can't be too careful. Code your references.'

Nick noted Black's change in attitude since they last met in Pristina. Something had sparked his interest and now he was more engaged.

'Okay,' Nick replied. 'What are we going to do about the difficult situation our solicitor is facing?'

'Do? Nothing. What can we do?'

'Well, I don't think we should abandon him to tackle

this trouble on his own.'

'Our friends in northern Cyprus and Macedonia are beyond our reach. We will just have to see how the game develops,' Black replied wearily.

'Given the threat, I think it is a rather serious game,' Nick persisted. 'We have a team member at risk.'

Their difference of opinion was partly a result of their training. The military was all about team work with the emphasis on the TOGETHER EVERYONE ACHIEVES MORE approach and although the SAS were more independent than the average soldier, they still valued friendship. MI6 agents, on the other hand, were trained to be objective. They looked at the cold, hard facts and nothing else. However, it was not just a matter of training. Personality traits come into play as well, although you could say that the institution chooses the character that best suits its own culture. If this be the case, with Simon Black, MI6 had chosen well.

Black turned away from the wall of marmalade jars and looked at Nick directly.

'I thought you, of all people, would understand about risk. Risk is not something to be avoided - it is something to be assessed. I wouldn't leap across a ditch at my age, in case I broke my leg, but when I was a child, playing in a field, I would happily leap back and forth over one. Risk is the bedfellow of ambition and by taking risks we achieve greater outcomes.'

'Not always,' Nick retorted. 'Anyway, it is not you taking the risk. You are putting someone else at risk.'

Black let out a long sigh indicating he was tired of having to explain himself to a colleague who ought to know better.

'I am assessing the risk and concluding that it is within the capabilities of our solicitor to handle this predicament. If not – it is a shame, but it is a risk we must take. I am hoping that this interlude may encourage our friends to travel to a jurisdiction where we can assist.'

'And in the meantime, we do nothing?'

'I am liaising with Interpol,' Black snapped and then bit his lip. Nick Rowe had rattled him. 'I am going to buy this now,' he said, selecting another jar of marmalade. 'I suggest you do the same. And follow the recipe. We want a good breakfast, not a dog's dinner.'

Ian finished the draft Inland Revenue account for Graham Tower's estate, looked up and saw Rita still sat at a desk in the corner. Holly and Ed had already gone home.

'What are you doing here? It's nearly 6pm.'

'You didn't tell me to go,' Rita replied.

'I'm sorry. I'm miles away. I've been concentrating on these valuations. We have everything now other than the figures for the Swiss bank account. I still haven't resolved that one.'

'You go to Switzerland?'

'Maybe, but right now I'm going home. Come on, I will give you a lift as you live in Ripon.'

They didn't talk much in the car as Ian was preoccupied, so he kept the conversation light. Ever since he had exchanged contracts, he had felt a sense of foreboding. He was waiting for Granville to react and, unusually for Ian, he was feeling anxious.

'I think I will run round Studley when I get home,' Ian said as they approached the outskirts of Ripon.

'Me too,' Rita replied. 'I might see you.'

It was virtually unheard of for Ian to stop running once he had started, but he was facing a strong westerly wind as he ran up the drive towards St Mary's church and his attention was grabbed by a kestrel which was flying parallel alongside him. Well, not quite because the kestrel was much higher but it had the same line of attack. It was flying directly into the wind, flapping its wings hard but also climbing very slowly - almost in slow motion. It made an unusual sight and Ian stopped to watch.

Eventually, the kestrel reached the height it wanted and then started to hover. Its tail was fanned and its wings were beating rapidly as it used every ounce of its strength to gain the advantage. Then it turned. A mouse had left a urine trail and the kestrel was able to identify the ultraviolet colours in the discharge. It had spotted its opportunity and with the wind now behind it, the kestrel dived for its prey. With its eyes fixed on the target, the kestrel struck and the mouse didn't stand a chance.

Ian marvelled at the sight. There was something suggestive about the uphill struggle being rewarded by the speed of the descent. He mulled over Harold's words about everything being reflected in nature, as he pressed on up the drive.

Rita wasn't far behind him. She had set off from King Edward Road, but Ian had made a later start, so now there were just a few hundred yards between them. He hadn't seen her, nor had he paid any attention to the Mercedes which had driven past him. Rita, however, had because she recognised the driver.

Valon stopped and let Ian run past the car. He had to make a detour around it, so he did notice the Mercedes now, but thought nothing of it. Cars often stopped so the occupants could observe the deer.

Rita had increased her pace and was running hard to close the gap but she was still some way behind.

Now that the target had been identified, Valon set off again to overtake Ian. He wasn't driving fast, perhaps 20 mph. Ian could hear the car behind him and tucked in slightly to the edge of the road. He had no reason to consider it a danger, but as Valon came alongside him, Granit pulled on the handle and kicked open the front passenger door, catching Ian in the back. Ian stumbled to the ground more shocked than injured.

Before Ian could gather his senses, Granit had jumped

out of the car and manhandled him by the top of his running shirt and waistband of his shorts into the back of the Mercedes. Ian was now face down across the back seat with Granit's meaty fingers clasped tightly around his neck.

Ian struggled to break free, but Granit sat across the back of his legs and forced Ian's face into the upholstery with his heavyset hands. Ian was only able to breathe intermittently, when he managed to raise his head a couple of inches.

Valon set off slowly, checking his mirrors to see what was behind him, as he approached the road on his left that led down to the lake. The idea was to slowly follow the one-way system, without drawing any attention to themselves, before taking Ian somewhere more private where they could dispose of him.

Rita had seen Ian being bundled into the car and veered off the driveway, taking a shortcut across the park. It imposed a steeper gradient up to a log bench at the top of the hill and a sharper downhill decline, but the route was more direct.

Trees lined the roadway down to the lake and fallen branches littered the grassland. Thinking on her feet, she picked up a log about four feet long and about as thick as a man's arm. The ground gave her a slight height advantage and as the Mercedes cruised up to her, she flung it at the windscreen. She scored a direct hit and the windscreen shattered into thousands of tiny pieces. Valon hit the brakes causing the Mercedes to swerve off the road towards her. His face was rammed into an airbag and his right hand slipped off the steering wheel and through the broken windscreen.

Granit was thrown into the back of the front passenger seat and lost his grip around Ian's neck as Ian's feet slid into the footwell.

Ian was unaware of Rita's involvement. He simply thought the car had hit something and skidded off the road. His one conviction was to escape. He knew where he was and he knew exactly where he wanted to go. He pulled on the door handle and dragged himself out of the car. Then he started running. Granit staggered out of the opposite side and began to follow but, being stout, at a slower pace.

Rita had picked up another piece of fallen oak, this one about two feet in length and a similar width to the first branch, but with a spikey end. She leapt on to the bonnet of the car and smashed it down on to Valon's hand like a fencing contractor ramming in a post. Valon let out a scream. His hand was already bleeding and now it was crushed and full of splinters. He pulled himself out of the car and as he did so Rita, still standing on the bonnet, whacked him on the back of the head, but not with much force. He stumbled to the ground with his face hitting the muddy gravel at the side of the road. He rolled on to his back just as Rita pounced on him. She stuck the log across his neck and pressed down on it as hard as she could.

Briefly, she had the upper hand but he was much stronger. He had a neck like a bull and the pressure she exerted seemed to have no effect. He put his hands at either ends of the log and sat up. Rita's back bent like a willow in the wind. They both grappled to their feet and Valon punched her with his right hand on the same cheek as her scar. He winced with pain as his fractured fist made contact with her cheekbone.

Rita was knocked to the ground. Granit straddled her back and grabbed her by the hair, forcing her face into the shallow, stone gutter. Surface water run-off was trickling down the hill winding its way through the loose gravel. Rita could hardly breathe and was choking on the water. She felt overpowered and thought there was nothing she could do. Her body was giving in but then she pictured her scar and remembered her vow.

She sucked up a mouthful of water mixed with gravel and slithered onto her back. She then blew out the contents of her mouth into Valon's eyes with all the power of projectile vomit. He reeled backwards but was still balanced on his knees as she jumped to her feet. She picked up the log and with the pirouette of a ballet dancer, smashed it against the side of his head. He fell like a tree struck by lightning.

Rita stood over him, still clutching the log. She didn't

want to kill him, but she wanted revenge. She wanted to scar his face like he had done to her, but then the moment passed. In that split second, she realised he wasn't worth it.

Valon was only just conscious. A slight groaning sound indicating that he was coming round. Rita knelt on one knee beside him.

'We are told an eye for an eye,' she said, 'but if I see you again, I will kill you.'

With that, she let go of the branch and ran. She headed back up the road towards the main driveway. She glanced back quickly and saw Granit in the distance. She could not see Ian and hoped he had escaped. She kept running as fast as she could. She wanted to burst into tears, but first she had to get home. Later, in the safety of her bedroom, she wept for an hour.

Ian ran for the café overlooking the lake, his heart pounding so fast it felt as though it was going to burst out of his chest. He pushed open the wrought iron gate, ran across the garden and vaulted the fence that separated the café from the grounds of Fountains Abbey. He was heading for Gertie's tunnel – somewhere to hide, but he realised Granit was following him. Ian was a good 100 yards ahead but Granit was too close to lose sight of him. Ian wanted to flee but realised he would have to fight.

A wooden footbridge spanned the River Skell at the top of the lake. Ian glanced behind and saw Granit was approaching the café. For a brief few seconds Ian would be out of sight, so he slipped into the water and lay under the bridge, his feet pointing towards the opposite bank and his head raised out of the water. Every muscle tightened as the cold water registered with his brain and his body prepared for action.

Within seconds Granit's heavy footsteps started reverberating on the wooden planks and Ian immediately sprung up and pulled Granit's ankles away from him. Granit plunged, head first, into the water downstream of the bridge, but he didn't fall into the lake. Ian had miscalculated. There was a good six feet gap between the downstream side of the bridge and the waterfall at the top of the lake, and this channel was barely a foot deep.

Ian scrambled over the bridge and grabbed Granit by his clothes, trying to drag him over the edge but he was too heavy. Granit raised himself on to his hands and knees and stood up. He lashed out and knocked Ian backwards so that he sat down in the water, but Ian, also, jumped back up. Granit threw a punch and then another but Ian avoided both. Being soaking wet, they were moving slowly. Ian staggered forward, grabbed Granit's sweatshirt near his collar and tried to pull him towards the edge, but Granit grasped Ian in a bear hug. He lifted Ian off the ground, squeezing the base of his back. Ian arched away in pain and Granit fell forwards, landing on top of him.

Ian was underwater now and Granit had him by the

throat, his beefy fingers crushing Ian's windpipe. Ian was running out of options. His strength was sapping away rapidly. He still had a grip around Granit's sweatshirt and tried to push up, but to no avail. Granit was like an immoveable rock. Ian let go. His arms dropped, outstretched to his side. Granit doubled down; sensing victory was near. Ian was barely moving now, just his right hand patting the riverbed. He felt a stone, angular but palm sized, almost pyramidal in shape. He gripped it at its base and lifting his arm, fully outstretched, he bashed it into the side of Granit's head with every ounce of strength he could muster. It knocked Granit off balance and he toppled to his side. Ian rolled onto his knees, gasping for breath. Granit was recovering his poise so Ian shuffled on his knees towards him and jabbed him on the forehead with the sharp point of the stone. Granit clutched his face with his hands to protect himself, but Ian stood up and stabbed the stone into the top of his head. He did it again and again until Granit dropped, dazed, face down in the water. Ian paused with exhaustion and relief, and then sat down in the water and, using both feet, he pushed him over the edge of the waterfall.

Ian crawled backwards, towards the footbridge and hoisted himself up, using the side of the bridge for support. He couldn't see Granit so he approached the front of the waterfall. He was worried he might have killed him, but Granit was flailing about in the silt, formed by centuries of duck and goose droppings, blood streaming from the top of his head.

Ian smiled at his victory but across the lake he could see Valon leaning against the crashed car. He didn't look like a threat, but what if they gathered themselves together and came after him?

Ian took some deep breaths. His heart was still racing and he was soaking wet. He decided to head for his original destination and hide until it was dark.

He crossed the river and started jogging towards the ruins of the Abbey and then doubled back as he climbed the steep hill towards Gertie's tunnel. Short of breath, he went inside and headed towards the centre. The light quickly diminished until he was completely in the dark. He was invisible from either end. He would hear anyone coming before they saw him. He would have time to react. He sank down on the bare, damp soil and, for a moment he felt safe. He didn't want to leave, but a chilling wind whispered through the tunnel and pierced his clothing. He was cold and he started shaking.

Chapter Twelve

Ian was shivering uncontrollably.

He stood up and moved to the front of the tunnel from where his elevated position gave him an advantage. He would be able to see Granit and Valon approach long before they reached him, so he dropped into a crouching position.

He wanted to stay in the tunnel. It felt safe and would give him time to think, but his involuntary shivering was becoming more violent. His clothes were soaking wet, but there was no point taking them off because he would have to sit there naked. He would just have to tough it out, he thought, but he was colder than he realised.

His plan was to wait until dark but at this time of year that could be another two to three hours. The sun was low on the horizon but it was glowing brightly, bathing everything in an orange light.

Suddenly, Ian felt a sharp stabbing pain on the right-hand side of his lower back. It was a deep, acute pain. He let out a groan and pressed his hand on the affected area. There was nothing to feel but the pain was really deep inside him and it was getting worse. He quickly realised he had to get home and reluctantly decided to make a move. He had just over a mile to go.

Ian walked unsteadily down the hill towards the river but he was still shivering. Actually, it was more of a sporadic judder. Strangely, he then started sweating.

When he reached the river bank, momentarily, he wasn't sure where he was. Everything looked different and he couldn't get his bearings. Landmarks seemed to be in the wrong place and too far away but luckily, he made the right turn and headed for the footbridge. By the time he got there the sweat was pouring off him and he was in agony. He knew he wouldn't make it back home.

Ian glanced across the lake and couldn't see the Mercedes. That was good, but he also realised that there was something seriously wrong. He needed to get to hospital. He could see a light glowing upstairs at the café and he decided to ask for help. He made it to the garden gate and collapsed onto the top bar; then slid himself over it and landed in a heap on the other side. He stumbled to the back door of the café and slapped it hard. There was no bell but it was an old, slightly ill-fitting, door so it clattered against the doorframe. No one stirred so Ian slapped it again, harder. Another light came on and he could hear footsteps. Eventually, the door opened a couple of inches. It was on a chain.

'Please help me,' Ian said, whilst trying to catch his breath. 'Ring 999. I need an ambulance.'

There was a woman behind the door. She hesitated. She could see he was in a bad way. The sweat was not forming beads on his brow; it was literally streaming down his face. Still, she was reluctant to open the door to a stranger.

'Please ring 999,' Ian repeated before his legs gave way and he collapsed in a heap on the ground.

The woman still had the door on its chain and she was peeping at Ian through the gap.

'I can't feel my legs below the knee,' Ian yelled anxiously. 'Or my arms below the elbows.'

Ian was panicking now. His body was shutting down. His brain was giving instructions to abandon the extremities so that the blood and oxygen could be concentrated on his core.

The woman opened the door. He could hardly be a threat in this condition.

Ian lay slumped in the doorway. He started hyperventilating. Sucking in as much oxygen as he could. He heard the woman on the phone.

She said: 'Ambulance,' and then he heard her give her name. 'Inga Gunnarsson,' she said, or something like that. Then she described, in a distressed manner, the situation before her and gave a postcode.

She came over to Ian. It was the first time he had seen her properly. He noticed she was wearing black silk pyjamas with ivory piping and had long, straight, ice blonde hair.

'I'm sorry,' he said. 'I don't know what's wrong with me. I can't feel my arms and legs.'

Ian was still breathing rapidly and sweating profusely. The deep breathing was the body's way of counteracting the pain. Inga stared at him, like a rabbit in the headlights, wondering what to do next and then she grabbed a tea towel from an oven rail. Ian noticed he was in the doorway of her kitchen.

'An ambulance is on its way,' Inga said, as she crouched down and wiped his face with the tea towel. She stayed kneeling at his side, occasionally dabbing his brow, until after a few minutes they heard a siren. It was close. Just one blast announcing its arrival.

She stepped over him and went outside, through the garden to the entrance gate. A green and white estate car had just pulled up and a paramedic jumped out carrying a case and backpack with him.

'Hi, I'm Chris,' he said. 'Where's the patient?'

'Hi, I'm Inga. This way please.'

She was only gone two or three minutes but, by the time they reached the kitchen, Ian was in the process of standing up. His face was relaxed. Not screwed up in agony as it had been when Inga had left him.

'I'm okay. I'm okay now,' he said, still wiping his face with the tea towel. 'The pain has just gone. Like turning off a light switch.'

'You don't look okay to me. I'm Chris, by the way. Now just sit yourself down here,' he said authoritatively, leading Ian to a small kitchen table.

'We'll have this off for a start,' he said, lifting Ian's running top over his head. 'You're soaking wet. Have you got a towel, Inga?' he asked, looking towards her, 'and a sweatshirt or something he can put on?'

Inga was still staring at Ian and noticed his muscular torso. Despite this current medical emergency, he was obviously fit.

'Yes, of course,' she replied, rousing herself into action.

Chris rubbed Ian down and took his pulse. He had stopped sweating, but was still shivering.

'And your name is?' he asked.

'Ian.'

'Well, Ian, your heart is racing. I'm going to take your blood pressure and then you can put this on.'

Inga had placed a sweatshirt on the kitchen table. It was black and after Chris had taken Ian's blood pressure, he helped him put it on. It was a little short, but otherwise seemed to fit quite well and it felt warm.

'Yes, your blood pressure is up. We're running on all cylinders this evening, aren't we? Now, how did you get so wet?'

'I fell in the river,' Ian replied.

'That would explain the immersion hypothermia but

not your other symptoms. Now, have we got some jogging bottoms to go with that sweatshirt, Inga?'

Inga went back upstairs and Chris held out the towel like a matador.

'Come on. We'll have those running shorts off please. I won't look, but there's nothing I haven't seen before,' he said cheekily as Inga came back down the stairs.

Ian thought Chris was a little fussy but he appreciated the care and attention. He wrapped the towel around his waist and slid off the running shorts. Inga threw some black jogging bottoms on to the table, not wishing to come too close, and Ian pulled them on over his wet socks and trainers.

'We'll have these off too please. Water conducts heat from the body 25 times faster than air.'

Ian sat back down and Chris started undoing the laces of his trainers. I think I've got some competition, Inga thought to herself.

'I'm feeling okay now,' Ian said. 'The pain has gone. I'll go home and have a hot bath.'

'No, you won't. You've got to warm up slowly from the inside. The next thing you need is a hot sugary drink. Is that something you could make for us Inga?'

'I've got some hot chocolate?'

'Perfect,' Chris replied.

'Do you want one as well?' Inga asked.

'No, just for the patient please, whilst I examine him.'

Ian was warming up. He was still cold but no longer shivering and the pain in his back had gone. The blessed relief from that pain put him on a high and he was talking excitedly, but Chris knew this was a reaction to a body pumped full of endorphins.

'Now, you say you experienced a sharp pain in your lower back, it was agony and then it went suddenly?'

'Yes.'

'Was the pain about here?' Chris asked, pressing on Ian's right kidney.

'Yes,' Ian moaned.

'Have you had a blow to your back? I can see a bruise developing.'

'I did get a bit of a knock to it earlier in the day,' Ian replied.

'Mmm. Well, you have mild hypothermia and I think, whilst suffering from that, you've passed a kidney stone. Aren't we a clever boy!'

'Crikey,' was all Ian replied. Then he stood up and said: 'I'd better get home.'

'Don't you underestimate what you've just been through,' Chris replied, giving Ian a stern look. 'Hypothermia occurs when the body loses heat faster than it can generate it. Eventually, the core is unable to maintain sufficient warmth to allow the proper function of the vital organs. Just as your hypothermia started, your body decided to pass a kidney stone which, apart from childbirth, is the most painful thing you can do. Your body went into overdrive and cut off blood and oxygen to everything but your core. That shows how close you were to something far more serious.'

Ian raised his eyebrows in surprise. 'So, what do I do now?' he asked.

'You go home, eat something warm and get to bed. No bath. Then tomorrow morning come to Ripon hospital and we will carry out some more tests. I will let them know to expect you.'

'Okay. Fine. Thank you,' Ian replied, giving staccato answers. 'Erm, can you give me a lift? I just live in the village at the bottom of the road.'

'Of course,' Chris replied.

Ian turned to face Inga.

'Thank you so much, Inga?'

'Yes,' she nodded.

'I'll bring these back as soon as,' he said, tugging at the sweatshirt.

'No problem,' she replied.

Sky was waiting up for Ian when he returned home and she was not best pleased by his late arrival. He let her out, made a mug of soup and went to bed. Usually, Sky slept in a basket on the landing, but she seemed to sense something was wrong. She jumped on the end of the bed and lay facing the door. It was her way of guarding him from intruders.

The next morning Ian attended Ripon hospital and was seen by Dr Holt who listened to Ian attentively and then asked for a urine sample. He had analysed it within a couple of minutes.

'You've got blood in your urine,' he said. 'I'll get you taken down to the X-ray department and when they are finished with you, bring the X-rays back to me.'

Ian did as he was instructed although he thought it slightly strange to be wandering up the hospital corridors carrying his own X-ray results.

Dr Holt clipped one of the X-rays to a screen with a light behind it and pointed to Ian's kidney.

'These light areas are kidney stones,' he said. 'What's happened is, one has become dislodged and made its way into your bladder. The pain is caused by the movement from the kidney to the bladder. It's like passing a pea through one of those little wires inside a plug. Once it reaches the bladder, the pain stops, but now we have to get it out.'

Ian looked white. 'How do we do that?' he gulped.

'With any luck it may happen naturally. The stone is like a gravelly ball and if you drink plenty of water it may gradually dissolve. It will hurt to pee for a while but that is better than intervention. The blood in your urine indicates this is already happening,' he said reassuringly.

'And you say there are more stones in my kidney?'

'Yes, but that's not necessarily a problem. They may

never move. I think the knock you had just sent this one on its journey.'

'I don't want to pass another one!' Ian exclaimed.

'No, it is extremely painful.'

'Right, so plenty of water,' Ian said, looking concerned. 'Anything else?'

'Go easy on the salt,' the doctor ordered.

Granit and Valon were licking their wounds and keeping a low profile. Both had minor head injuries, Granit's worse than Valon's, but Valon's right hand was also badly swollen. It looked strange. Like something unnatural on the end of his arm.

'Hello, boss,' Granit said when Spartak answered his telephone.

'Granit?' Spartak replied.

'Yes. I'm afraid we didn't kill the lawyer. Sorry boss. He got away,' Granit said sheepishly.

'Why kill the lawyer?'

'Mr Frederick. He told us to,' Granit explained.

'You should take your orders from me. I haven't asked for the lawyer to be killed,' Spartak replied curtly.

'You have Russian woman now. You gave us to Mr Frederick.' Spartak sensed the hurt in Granit's voice and softened his approach.

'I lent you to Mr Frederick. Polina is just a personal bodyguard. You are my business managers and I need you back here. The NATO bombing has worked and now the Serbs are fleeing for their lives. Russia won't do anything because Yeltsin doesn't want to fight a proxy war with the United States, so it is time for us to re-establish our territory.'

'And the lawyer?' Granit asked.

'Leave him to me. It's time for you to come home.'

'Yes, boss,' Granit replied happily.

Ian left the hospital and went to Ripon Police Station. He gave the desk sergeant a brief, watered-down version of events mainly to cover his back in case someone else reported something. Then he went to get some flowers for Inga as a thank you for her help.

It was a lovely day and Ian needed a bit of time out of the office. First, however, he thought he'd better telephone Holly to say he would be late. He wasn't going to worry her with any details, but when she answered the phone, he immediately sensed the anxiety in her voice.

'Ian, are you okay?'

'Yes, I'm fine but how do you know what's been happening?'

'Rita has told us all about it.'

'Rita?'

'Yes. She saved you. She threw a log at the car and broke the windscreen and then she fought that man Valon and beat him.'

'Gosh. I didn't even know she was there.'

'She saw you running off and Granit running after you, but then she said she saw Granit on his own so she assumed you had got away.'

'Yes, I did. Is she okay?'

'Yes, she's all right,' Holly confirmed. 'At least, I think she is.'

'Well, please thank Rita on my behalf and say I will be in shortly to do so personally. Firstly, however, I've got a little job to do.'

'Okay, we'll see you later, and Ian.'

'Yes.'

'Be careful.'

Ian popped into the flower shop but struggled with the selection. He liked the white and yellow roses but somehow, he didn't think Inga would be so keen, although he knew nothing about her. They had some red roses but, regrettably, Ian thought they would be inappropriate, so he settled on some pink peonies. Armed with these he headed for the café.

'She's not in,' a man shouted when he heard Ian tapping at Inga's door. It was the manager of the café and he had come out to see what Ian was doing when he saw him walk around the back.

'You wouldn't know when she will be back would you?' Ian asked.

The man noticed the flowers in Ian's hand.

'No, but she only works up at Fountains Hall. You can go and see her there if you wish.'

'Thank you,' Ian replied.

Ian spun the Jag round and headed for Fountains Hall. As the crow flies it was barely a mile but by car, Ian had to drive back through Studley Roger, up Pateley Bridge Road and then through the village of Aldfield to what he always thought of as the back entrance to Fountains Abbey. During this four-mile journey he felt both nervous and excited.

Fountains Hall was a Grade I listed manor house within the grounds of the Abbey, but Ian had no idea what it was currently used for. He went through the front door, saw a rather efficient looking lady walking towards some stairs and asked her if it would be possible to see Inga.

'Perhaps,' she replied and carried on walking up the stairs.

Ian felt he was left hanging in the air and was wondering whether to leave when Inga appeared at the top of the staircase and walked towards him. She was wearing a black pencil-shaped dress, pinched at the waist with a narrow belt. The dress had a round neck, three-quarter length sleeves and fell just below the knee. Accompanied by barely black tights and black court shoes, it formed a stark contrast to her ice blonde hair and she looked dramatically attractive.

'Hello, I've brought you these,' Ian said. 'As a thank

you for last night.'

The efficient looking lady reappeared and raised her eyebrows.

'Thank you,' Inga replied, taking the flowers.

Ian noticed she was wearing dark nail varnish.

'I'm sorry for any inconvenience,' he said awkwardly.

'Not at all. Are you fully recovered now?'

'Yes, fighting fit,' Ian replied.

'Good. I'm pleased,' Inga said, a little stiltedly.

'Yes, right, well thank you again,' Ian said. 'Good-bye.'

'Good-bye,' she replied.

They both turned away and then Ian called across the hall:

'Oh, and I will pop your tracksuit back to the café.'

Inga glanced back at him, gave a sort of nod, and carried on towards the stairs.

Chapter Thirteen

It was one of those surreal moments. When Ian arrived at the office, Dr Holt was stood in reception talking to Holly. He was accompanied by a woman and they turned towards Ian as he entered.

Ian hesitated. He knew the face, but it was in the wrong place! He had only met Dr Holt a few hours ago and now he had changed from medical gown to blazer, and was waiting for Ian at his place of work.

'This is Dr Anthony Holt and his wife Miss Rachel Armfield,' Holly said, seeing the look of surprise on Ian's face. 'They want to buy a house.'

'Yes, of course. Forgive me. I just had one of those out of context moments,' Ian said as he proffered his hand.

'My fault. I should have made an appointment, but my wife has just arrived by train from Leeds, and we wanted to see a solicitor together whilst we had the chance. Rachel is a consultant surgeon hence the Miss and, for work, she uses her maiden name,' Dr Holt replied, whilst shaking Ian's hand.

'How do you do?' Rachel said, also giving Ian a firm handshake. She was slim and elegant looking with the demeanour of a confident professional.

'Please forgive my husband's lack of protocol but I work out of Leeds General Infirmary, mainly, and it is difficult for us to synchronise our diaries. We hope to buy this house in Burn Bridge which will work well for both of us from a commuting perspective.'

'Not at all,' Ian replied, looking at the sales particulars which she had just handed to him. 'Would you like to come through to the meeting room?'

'You lead the way,' Dr Holt replied.

They made themselves comfortable and Ian started flicking through the sales particulars. The property was called Horn Beck House and it was situated just off Brackenthwaite Lane which was known locally as Millionaires' Row. It appeared to be a beautifully renovated, stone farmhouse set in landscaped gardens which sloped gently down to Horn Beck. There was a picturesque, Japanese style, wooden bridge over the beck which led to a summer house set in front of a strand of woodland trees. The front of the summer house faced the beck and the rear garden.

'Beautiful property,' Ian said admiringly. 'I'll get on with it straight away.'

'I knew you would,' Dr Holt responded. 'I said to Rachel, anyone who can pass a kidney stone and turn up to work the next morning must have balls of steel.'

Rachel slapped her husband's knee with the back of

her hand. 'Tony,' she said with a mocking exasperation.

'Have you anything to sell?' Ian asked.

'Rachel has a flat in Leeds and we jointly own a terraced house in Harrogate. We'll have to sell both to fund this place,' Tony said, pointing at the picture of the new property on the front of the sales particulars.

'And what about a mortgage?'

'We've got a broker looking into it. I'll give him your details.'

'Excellent. Well, I think we are good to go,' Ian said as he stood up and led them back through reception. He made a point of introducing them to Ed and Rita and they had, of course, already met Holly.

'We work as a team,' Ian said, 'so if I am not available, any of my colleagues will be able to help you.'

'I suggest we meet at the casino again,' Spartak had said to Granville. 'Matters are too serious to discuss over the telephone.'

It was just as well, given that GCHQ were listening to all Granville's calls but, nevertheless, Granville would rather not have met Spartak in person. He knew that Spartak's 'suggestion' was a demand and he was cognisant of Spartak's initial warning, so he sat waiting, nervously hoping he could avoid his fate.

Granville had noticed Polina in the bar, but he was too distracted to see Spartak's entrance. Without warning, he simply appeared in front of him.

'Drink?' Granville asked as he looked up at Spartak in surprise. He hadn't dared to order champagne, so he raised his glass of raki an inch or so off the table by way of recommendation. Beads of condensation were running down the outside of the glass. Spartak slapped a card on the table next to Granville's drink as he sat down. It was the ace of spades.

'Next time you see this, it will be pinned to your chest,' Spartak snarled, towering over him.

'No need for that,' Granville blustered. 'I'm sure we can sort it out.'

'By killing the lawyer? Just how does that resolve anything? Does that get me my money back?'

Granville stared at his drink. 'No,' he replied quietly.

'So how are you going to get my money back?'

'Well, we haven't lost it yet,' Granville said, his demeanour suddenly lifting. 'We still have time to complete, if you can invest the balance of the money.' The impetus of his words declined as he finished his sentence.

'I don't have that sort of ready cash and I wouldn't give it to you if I had. It's your problem. You sort it out.'

'I don't have the ready cash either,' Granville pleaded.

Spartak sat down next to Granville and put an arm around his shoulder as though he was comforting a child.

'You have risked £300,000 of my cash and you must pay it back. Then we are even. I will give you two weeks,' he said, squeezing him tightly.

Granville was perspiring now and Spartak released his grip as he saw a wet patch reflect an image of Granville's spine down the back of his shirt. Granville knew the consequences of default and made one last desperate throw of the dice.

'I need your help,' he said. 'To sort all this out. Sutherland must have exchanged contracts for a reason. He knew he would lose your money. Who is he really working for? Maybe it is part of a secret plan to trap you?'

Granville was grasping at straws now, trying to think of some intricate plot that he could conjure up to convince Spartak that Ian was to blame. He started warming to his subject.

'Think about it. I was only doing what I had done before. Giving the lawyer a deposit and then asking for it back. I had no idea he would exchange and he had no authority to do so. I don't gain from this. Who does? Let's work out who does.' Granville was virtually panting, looking up at Spartak like a spaniel awaiting its master's command.

Spartak observed him carefully without saying anything. Eventually, he broke the tension.

'We need to speak to this lawyer then, not kill him. Not yet.'

'Yes, I agree,' Granville spluttered. 'I acted too hastily. I was so angry, on your behalf.' Again, his enthusiasm trailed as he uttered the last few words and Spartak could tell he was lying.

'Don't bullshit me! You're not off the hook yet. One of you will pay - I just haven't decided which one yet.'

'No, of course. You're absolutely right and you will see this is Sutherland's fault. I will prove it to you,' Granville said, like a man reprieved.

'Who could this Sutherland be working for?' Spartak mused.

'Ryan Curtis?' Granville suggested. 'You did have him thrown off a bridge and tried to take his business. Or have you any enemies in England? Kosovan competitors who have employed him? Or are the police on to you or one of the secret services?'

'Ryan Curtis doesn't have the balls,' Spartak replied 'and my competitors would fight me on their territory not in England. Plus, this is too sophisticated. No, if he is working for someone, it must be the CIA or MI6. Someone like that.'

'Exactly!' Granville said triumphantly. 'Sutherland has nothing to gain either. The CIA or MI6 must be trying to flush you out.'

'So, I must think, what would they expect me to do and then I will do the opposite. In the meantime, set up a meeting with Sutherland.' Spartak stood up to leave.

'Will do,' Granville replied. 'I'll come up with a plan and think about everything very carefully.'

'And keep the card,' Spartak said. 'Someone's going to wear it.'

'Come on Rita,' Ian said, a couple of days after receiving instructions from Dr Holt and Miss Armfield. 'I'll take you to Burn Bridge and show you what a proper conveyancing solicitor does.'

They set off in the E-type, Rita sitting quietly and somewhat apprehensively in the passenger seat.

'I wanted to thank you for what you did at Studley the other day,' Ian said. 'It was very brave of you.'

'I just reacted to the situation,' Rita replied. 'Granit and Valon are bad men. Valon did this to me (she pointed at her scar) and I wanted revenge but when it came to it, once the threat to you was over, how do you say, my appetite went.'

'I didn't even know you were there, otherwise I wouldn't have left you.'

Rita looked embarrassed or, perhaps, a little self-conscious.

'No, it took real guts to do what you did and I will always be grateful,' Ian said, giving her an affirming smile.

'I wanted revenge. I was driven by hate, but I'm not bothered anymore.' She hesitated: 'but I still want justice. I can't explain it. I want him to be punished but I no longer want to hurt him myself. Does this mean I am a coward?'

'No,' Ian replied, in a long-drawn-out way of emphasizing the negative. 'It means you have matured. Revenge is when you take it upon yourself to get even. Justice is when you trust the powers that be to restore fair play. I am sure Valon will get his comeuppance in the end and it is best to leave that to others, but you are the bravest woman I know.'

'Brave but no longer beautiful,' she said sadly. 'Now I prioritise my career because no man will ever want me.'

'That's not true!' Ian exclaimed. 'You have an inner beauty. A pureness of spirit that shines through and makes you radiant. Any man that recognises that will never even notice your scar.'

Rita smiled bashfully and her eyes filled with tears. 'Thank you,' she said quietly, as she concentrated her gaze towards the footwell.

They arrived at Horn Beck House and knocked on the front door. The vendor, a Mr Butler, opened it.

'Hello, I'm Ian…'

'You're the solicitor,' Mr Butler interrupted. 'Well go round the back. The front door is for friends and family,' he said, slamming the door shut.

Rita looked at Ian in surprise. 'Don't worry about it,' Ian said.

The back door was, in fact, at the side of the house and by the time Ian and Rita approached, Mr Butler was stood there with the door open. He was of retirement age and dressed in blue shorts and a white linen shirt, turned up at the cuffs.

'Come in and sit there,' he said gruffly, pointing at the kitchen table. 'I will go and get my wife.'

The kitchen table was strewn with sales particulars and whilst Ian and Rita were left alone Ian had a quick glance at them. He noticed that the sale prices were all less than half the value of the house they were selling. There were also dozens of wine bottles, unopened, lined up by a door which seemed to lead to a cellar and Ian noticed that some of the labels looked damaged.

'Right, what is it you want to see?' Mr Butler demanded when he returned with his wife. 'If you're worried about flooding, the house is built near a natural spring and it's only the cellar that occasionally suffers from rising water. A rill was created over a hundred years ago to run through the cellar to keep it cool, but if there is a flash flood, it can rise too quickly. It soon settles down again though, so it's not a problem.'

'Except for the wine,' Ian said, tilting his head in the direction of the wine bottles.

'Oh, it's marvellous,' Mrs Butler replied hastily. 'Edmund has claimed for the wine on our house insurance, but the insurance company doesn't want to collect the bottles and there's nothing wrong with them. Just a bit of damage to the labels.'

Mr Butler glared at her. She was a plump woman,

wearing pink shorts and a loose fitting, pale blue cotton blouse patterned with white flowers. She looked as though she enjoyed a glass or two of Chardonnay.

'So, what do you want to see?' Mr Butler asked, spitting out the words.

'Nothing inside the house. I just want to walk the boundaries,' Ian replied.

'Oh, that's a relief!' Mrs Butler exclaimed. 'I mean, it's such a mess with us packing to leave.'

Mr Butler glared at her again. 'Well, it sounds like a waste of time to me,' he barked. 'Our solicitor never looked round when we bought it and we've lived here for twenty years. Why don't they just take our word for it instead of sending you to snoop around?'

'No one has sent me Mr Butler. I am just doing my job and I made an appointment through your estate agent so it shouldn't be a surprise. I also informed your solicitor that I would be coming to have a look at certain things so I have followed all the usual protocols.'

'What things?'

'Well, I can't discuss that. It would be against Law Society regulations as you would be deemed a weaker, unrepresented party. Any concerns I have will be raised with your solicitor and he will discuss them with you.'

Mr Butler's face went puce with anger. 'Well get on with it then,' he said, as he saw them out of the kitchen door and slammed it behind them.

'I loved the bit about weaker party,' Rita said as they walked down the garden together. She was almost skipping.

'He's going to regret his behaviour,' Ian replied.

They walked down to the bridge and then crossed the beck and sat on a garden bench outside the summerhouse.

'Look at them!' Mr Butler shouted at his wife as he spied through his binoculars. 'They'll get a picnic out next! I'm going to write a letter of complaint to our solicitor. In fact, no. I will report him to the Law Society.'

Ian pulled the Land Registry plan from his file and showed it to Rita.

'Look at this. The red edging marks the boundaries. Look at the position of the southern boundary,' Ian said, pointing at the plan with his index finger. Rita didn't say anything.

'The northern side of the beck forms the boundary to the property. Can you see? So, the Butlers have put a bridge over the beck and formed what the sales particulars describe as a wild garden on land they don't own.'

Rita took a sharp intake of breath. 'So, what does this mean?' she asked.

'It looks like they've encroached on to the neighbour's property and the neighbour appears to be a farmer who is only ploughing his land to the other side of those trees so maybe he's never noticed.'

'So, what will you do?'

'Make them pay,' Ian replied.

They walked back towards the house and Ian could see Mr Butler waiting outside the back door so he took a slightly wider berth than needed. He knew Mr Butler would want to quiz him and that it would irritate him if he left without saying anything.

'Thank you,' Ian shouted, raising an arm to wave good-bye. He could almost see Mr Butler saying: 'But...'

On the journey back to the office Ian gave Rita a résumé.

'So, we have learnt three things,' he said. 'One, they are hard up; two, Mr Butler is willing to defraud his insurance company, which says something about his character and three, they have a title problem. When we get back to the office, I would like you to ring Dr Holt and ask him to make an appointment for him and his wife to come and see me as soon as possible.'

Rita was thrilled.

Chapter Fourteen

'Thank God it's the weekend,' Ian murmured to Sky when he woke up on Saturday morning.

He made a cafetière of coffee, did some jobs around the house and about midday set off with Sky towards the café by the lake, to return Inga's clothes.

Sky was ten now and moved more slowly. The carpal joints on her front legs were swollen with arthritis, but it was a lovely sunny day and Ian was happy to go at her pace. About halfway up the drive, however, he saw Inga walking down the hill towards him.

He must have been looking at the ground because the first thing he saw was her black wet-look leggings and biker boots. As his eyes travelled upwards, he noticed her hair wafting over her shoulders in the breeze and her black vest-top with a dark grey design on the front.

'Hi! Fancy seeing you! I was just coming to your place to bring these back,' Ian said, lifting a bag in which he had placed her clothes.

'I was coming to see you too,' she said. 'I didn't thank you properly for the flowers. I'm sorry I had to be brief but people were watching.'

Ian was aware that he was still smiling broadly and he realised that he found Inga highly attractive. He didn't break eye contact and neither did she as they subconsciously made their assessments. Her make-up was unusual but alluring. A black eyeliner and deep mauve eyeshadow made her brown eyes look amazing; matched with a deep mauve lipstick, Ian was transfixed.

For a second, there was an awkward pause while Ian thought how to avoid bringing the conversation to a close by simply returning the clothes.

'Well, would you like to come back to my place for a quick coffee?' Ian said, in an anxious attempt to prolong the encounter. 'I live just around the corner.'

'Sounds lovely,' Inga replied.

Ian was a little apprehensive as they walked down the drive together. He estimated Inga was about twenty-five and he had never dated anyone that much younger than himself before. It made him feel a little constrained.

Inga said she had studied archaeology at York University and was temporarily employed by the National Trust to help with a project at Fountains Abbey – hence why she was living above the lakeside café.

'So, how come you are working in Fountains Hall?' Ian asked. 'I thought you would be digging up the ruins.'

'I'm cataloguing a previous excavation,' Inga laughed. 'I like studying human activity through the analysis of historical artefacts.'

As they approached Ian's cottage a man, digging in his garden, stood up and offered Ian a cauliflower.

'Would you like this?' he asked, holding it aloft like a football. 'These cauliflowers have taken me six months to grow from seed and now they've all come at once.'

'Thank you,' Ian replied.

'Who's that?' Inga whispered.

'That's Steve, my dentist.'

They went inside and Ian let Sky off the lead. She shot upstairs, not overly impressed by Inga, perhaps as she had paid little attention to her.

'I think I will cook this for lunch,' Ian said, putting the cauliflower beside the kitchen sink. 'Cauliflower cheese only takes ten minutes.'

'You can't cook that in ten minutes!' Inga retorted.

'You can watch me if you like.'

'Go on then,' she countered.

Ian put the oven on, chopped the cauliflower in half and gave it a good wash in cold water. He put some butter in a pan and as it melted, stirred in plain flour to make a roux. Then he added some watered-down, semi-skimmed milk and after it had simmered for a couple of minutes, took it off the heat and added a teaspoon of Dijon mustard and the cheese. Next, he spooned about a quarter of the sauce into a baking dish and added some florets of cauliflower. Then, he added the rest of the sauce and grated some parmesan over the top before placing it in the oven.

'Right, I'm setting the timer for ten minutes,' Ian said triumphantly.

'I thought it took more like twenty-five,' Inga replied.

'Not when it's fresh and at room temperature.'

Inga was watching him carefully. 'You're not married then?'

'Married! No.'

'Girlfriend?' Inga could have bitten her lip when she said this but it just came out and, unfortunately, Ian did look a little embarrassed.

'Not at the moment,' he replied cheekily.

'I'm sorry,' Inga said, trying to recover the situation. 'It is just that not many men are so adept in the kitchen.'

'Well, I did live with someone, briefly, but she was German and moved back home.'

'I'm half Swedish,' Inga retorted.

'That explains the blonde hair,' Ian said, in a way which made it clear he considered this an asset. 'My first crush was Agnetha Fältskog.' Then he added: 'the blonde from ABBA,' in case the reference was too historical.

Inga laughed. 'I think it has more to do with L'Oréal than my Swedish origins.'

Ian poured a glass of Sauvignon Blanc and passed it to her.

'Just something to freshen the palette,' he said.

The timer bleeped, Ian took the cauliflower cheese out of the oven and cut a couple of thick slices of bread from a Bettys granary loaf.

'Lunch is served,' he said with a flourish, handing Inga a plate of cauliflower cheese, a sliced tomato, and a chunk of bread.

'Impressive,' Inga replied, as she sat down at the kitchen table. 'The German girl doesn't realise what's she's missing!'

'My thoughts entirely,' Ian concurred.

'So, what went wrong, if you don't mind me asking?'

'Well, she went back to Munich and I followed her but when I got there, she already had another boyfriend, even though we had only been apart for a few weeks. He was a weedy little chap with a patchy beard and when I saw him, I just thought, if that's the competition I'm not interested, so I came home.'

'Understandable,' Inga said reassuringly.

Ian sat down opposite Inga noticing some of the finer details of her accessories. She wore a thin silver choker around her neck with a small ring hanging from its centre. It made a good connection between her blonde hair and black vest top. She started eating using a fork, American style, and rested her left arm on the table. Her nails were painted gun-metal grey and she had a black woven leather bracelet on her left wrist with a silver clasp. She looked seductive.

'Is that a Hermes bracelet?' Ian asked, recognising the signature H-clasp.

'Yes,' she replied, automatically giving her wrist a twist.

Ian touched her wrist with his fingertips so that the underside of her arm remained facing upwards.

'What's this?' he asked, looking at some faint scars which ran horizontally across the lower part of her arm.

She pulled away and folded her arms in a defensive position.

'Nothing,' she said.

Ian raised his eyebrows in a disbelieving sort of way.

'Okay, I used to self-harm,' she replied abruptly.

'Oh, no!' Ian exclaimed, screwing his face up at the thought of the self-inflicted pain. 'Why would you do that?'

'I liked watching it heal,' she responded factually.

Momentarily, they looked into each other's eyes. Ian searching for answers, Inga asking herself if she could trust him.

'But you didn't try to kill yourself?' he asked, with obvious stress in his voice.

'No,' Inga replied, looking down at her arm. 'I just made some shallow cuts with a razor blade. My psychiatrist explained it as the physical release of emotional pain.'

'But why did you do it?'

'My parents were getting divorced and it was very messy. My father was unfaithful and during the proceedings it came out that he was perverted as well. Violent actually.

He used to physically abuse his girlfriends.'

'He didn't hurt you though?'

Inga let out a sarcastic laugh. 'Hurt, yes but he wasn't physically violent with me. He just broke my heart. My whole world collapsed.'

'I'm sorry,' Ian said, stroking her arm gently.

'He ended up going to prison. I was only fifteen at the time and I suppose it was just my way of coping – or not – a sort of cry for help.'

'But you're okay now?' Ian asked anxiously.

'Yes,' she laughed. 'It was a long time ago.'

They were silent for a short time, still looking into each other's eyes.

'So, is your father Swedish?' Ian asked, to reignite the conversation.

'No, it is my mother who is Swedish. My father is English.'

'Oh, sorry, but you said your surname was Gunnarsson?'

'Yes, that's my mother's name. We reverted to that after the divorce.'

Ian was conscious that he had asked a lot of personal questions so he tried to change the subject.

'So, how's the cauliflower cheese?'

'Perfect,' Inga replied. 'You can't make a cheese soufflé by any chance, can you? It's my favourite.'

'No but I know someone who can. There is this

gastro pub in East Witton called The Blue Lion. It's their signature dish. We could go there for dinner sometime if you like?'

'Sounds lovely,' Inga said with a smile, echoing a phrase she had used earlier.

Now that was sorted, the intensity of the conversation eased into small talk. Inga finished her lunch and said good-bye with a gentle kiss to Ian's cheek - like a seal of approval, Ian thought. He didn't like the whole self-harming thing but it was understandable. What he didn't appreciate, was that some scars run deep.

'Sorry to be so dramatic but I wanted to show you this in person,' Ian said, as he sat down with Dr Holt and Miss Armfield in the café adjacent to Harrogate train station.

'No, it's good of you to meet us at 8am on a Monday morning,' Dr Holt replied.

'I am sorry,' Rachel interjected, 'but I must get to LGI for 9.30am at the latest. I'm operating so you've got 20 minutes.'

'Okay,' Ian said, clearing some space and laying out the Land Registry plan on the light grey, laminate-topped table.

'This red line marks the southern boundary of Horn Beck House. You will see it stops this side of the beck. So, the Butlers don't actually have title to what they call the wild garden and, therefore, they have built the summerhouse on someone else's land.'

Both doctors stared at the plan. 'Couldn't they claim, what's it called, possessory title or something?' Dr Holt queried.

'Not in this case. If the land was unregistered and the Butlers had incorporated it into their own boundaries to the exclusion of others, then they could, over time, acquire a possessory title, but the beck and all the land to the south of it is already registered to a local farmer.'

'So, what do we do now? Rachel asked.

'I think you've got three options. You could withdraw from the purchase.'

'We don't want to do that!' Dr Holt exclaimed.

'No, or we could delay matters until they sort it out.'

'How would they do that?' Rachel asked anxiously.

'Well, they could buy the land from the farmer or enter into a long lease, for instance.'

'That could take months!' she said exasperatedly.

'Yes, so my preferred option is to get the property revalued on the basis that the wild garden and the summerhouse are excluded. Then you lower your offer to reflect the new valuation. If the farmer lets you carry on using his land, you consider that a bonus.'

Rachel looked at her husband for confirmation and then said: 'We agree. The third option please.'

'Very good. I'll get on with it.'

'Can you arrange the revaluation and everything?'

Rachel asked.

'Of course,' Ian replied.

'Thank you,' Rachel said as she touched his hand.

Ian put down the telephone and went through to reception. He asked Ed to follow him and Rita was already there. He plonked down in a chair.

'I've just got off the phone with Granville's Bank and they are adamant that they will not give me any information unless I turn up in person. So, I am going to have to go to Zurich with the account number and password to find out how much is in the account.'

'Could that be dangerous?' Holly asked, looking concerned.

'I don't see why,' Ian replied. 'The police said that Granit and Valon fled the country the day after our little debacle so, presumably, they are back in Kosovo and I doubt Granville will try anything himself. He probably won't even realise I'm there. Anyway, if he does, I'll be ready for him.'

Holly rolled her eyes at this stupid male bravado.

'It's not a laughing matter,' Ed said.

'No, I appreciate that but whilst I am away, I am leaving you two in charge and Rita, I thought you might like to stay on and work for us during your summer holidays?'

'Really?' she chimed.

'Yes, and we'll pay you. Not a lot, but we will work

something out.'

Rita clapped her hands which Ian took to be a 'yes' and he went back to his desk to brief Mrs Towers.

You would think that some water would pass under the bridge before Granville found out; that it would take at least a few hours for the jungle drums to beat their message, but by the time Ian had finished speaking with Mrs Towers, Granville was on the phone to Spartak.

'Sutherland is going to Zurich,' Granville said. 'We could take care of him there.'

'How do you know?'

'Because he's just telephoned my bank in Zurich! The gods are smiling on us Spartak! As luck would have it, Sutherland acts for one of our investors who has just died. Sutherland has contacted the bank and given his name, the client's name, and the account number. As anonymity has been breached and as I am only one of three people entitled to know the identity of the investor, I was informed.'

'And why is he going to Zurich?'

'To access the account. That's the whole point. He must put in the account number and the password himself. The staff can't give him the information over the telephone. Not because they don't want to - they don't know it themselves.'

Granville had used his words carefully. He could have said: 'deal with' but that would imply a two-way negotiation which was not the intention; or, he could have said: 'meet' but that would indicate a willingness on Ian's part to participate which again was not the intention. He did not use anything more sinister such as 'dispose of' because he knew it was not Spartak's intention to harm Ian at this stage, but when Nick Rowe read the transcripts from GCHQ, he came to a different interpretation. Nick read 'take care of' in the context of Granville's earlier conversation with Granit and he was deeply concerned on Ian's behalf. He sent a coded message to Simon Black.

'I need some jam.'

It was the height of the tourist season and Fortnum & Mason was packed, but Black still stood out like a sore thumb as he meandered around the jams, marmalades, preserves and conserves section. Nick smiled to himself as he sidled up to him. Black wanted to look incognito, but why would a man close to retirement age, in horned-rimmed spectacles, grey flannel trousers and a tweed jacket spend so much time considering his breakfast options? And do so, regularly? Nick knew that the best way to go unobserved was to look like everyone else. To have no distinguishing features. To blend in was how he had been trained. 'Matching,' they called it. There was a human pre-disposition to do this as it made you part of the pack. That is why everyone that went to Glastonbury dressed in shorts and wellies and wore silly hats and it was why people that went fishing and shooting clothed themselves in tweed. Black was too awkward for all of that, but there again, looking around, the customers were a diverse lot. Maybe Black didn't stick out too much after all, Nick reassured himself.

'Have you seen the latest?' Nick asked, saying as little as possible.

'I have,' Black replied.

'Well, we can't let him go to Zurich.'

'Why not? This might be the opportunity we have been waiting for.'

'It might be dangerous,' Nick protested.

'Yes, you're right,' Black replied, always trying to give the impression of agreement even if he was exercising passive dominance. 'That's why I want you to go there to keep a close eye on things.'

'Have you alerted Interpol?'

'No, but I will.'

Nick wasn't so sure. Black was being very non-committal about everything, as usual. Switzerland was a neutral country and Granville owned one of its banks. Black might take a minimalist approach. However, his instructions were ambiguous. He had implied Nick should follow Ian and watch from a distance. Nick had a better idea.

Chapter Fifteen

Sometimes people can't cope. Pressure builds, anxiety attacks and a low mood sets in. They think they are managing. They are aware of the issues and feel they can carry on but then their body takes over. The mind is willing but the flesh is weak.

Ian had learned the hard way that in such situations you have to listen to your body, no matter how frustrating this might be at the time.

For Ian, his bête noire came in the form of a migraine. It always crept up on him unexpectedly, when least convenient, usually after a crisis, when the adrenalin rush was over and he was looking forward to something more enjoyable.

The worst thing was he could see them coming – like a train arriving at a station. They started with a tension across his brow. A tiredness that made him yawn repeatedly and a loss of colour to his face.

Every time he had the same reaction. He hoped it wouldn't arrive, but every time it did and stage two would see him curled up in bed, a black cloud of pain in his head. Sometimes, it was so bad he wanted to die, but he knew if he could hang on it would pass. It could take up to 36 hours, from start to finish, but he knew, eventually, often after vomiting violently, it would go away.

Stage three was the recuperation. The pain goes but a dullness descends. An exhaustion from which the body needs to recover. Plenty of water, fresh air and doing what you enjoy was the remedy. Nothing too vigorous but a 'time out' to recalibrate. Go back to work too soon and another one would be waiting around the corner.

Such was the reason Ian could not be found. Not even Nick Rowe could contact him. He was in a wood, near West Tanfield, with a fishing rod in one hand and Sky's lead in another.

The Tanfield Angling Club leased seven and a half miles of the River Ure between West Tanfield and Grewelthorpe, most of it running through a heavily wooded valley. The landlord and owner of the local estate was a farsighted steward and, in terms of conservation, decades ahead of his time, so Ian was in a natural paradise with no mobile phone connection and no other humans around. If anyone did draw near – the wildlife would herald their approach.

Ian laid his Barbour jacket on the ground and sat Sky next to it – an old trick shown to him by a gillie on the Tweed. Sky would be comforted by his scent on the jacket and she would stay put to guard it. Knowing Sky, however, he also gave her a chew which he hoped would distract her from the surrounding temptations. Then he started fishing, casting a dry fly upstream and watching it drift down over the feeding trout sipping emerging nymphs as they approached the surface film of the water.

Frustratingly, the trout were not really playing fair, refusing every imitation offered, until, at last, a fat two-pounder succumbed to a Griffiths gnat.

It fought hard but Ian won the battle and brought it to the net. He noticed it had a black mark above its left eye, the size of a fingernail and a hole in its back, revealing raw flesh, probably caused by a peck from a predator. Ian thought it might be kinder to kill it but instead, carefully withdrew the hook and released it. He checked on Sky and then cast again. Wow, a second take! This time the fish didn't fight much at all and Ian dragged it in only to discover it was the same fish! Its greed had overcome its experience.

Ian started to feel hungry and knew this was a sign that the migraine was over. Euphoria at the release from pain lifted his spirits and he headed home. There was a message on the answerphone to call Nick Rowe, but Ian decided to cook something first and call Nick tomorrow.

Frederick Granville was not so patient. Sutherland had asked his bank for information and his request had been refused. Indeed, he had been told that it would be against Swiss law to reveal it. Granville knew, therefore, that Sutherland would have to visit the bank in person, but he had no idea when this would be. Consequently, the practicalities of getting Spartak and Sutherland together were proving difficult. He tried to explain this to Spartak.

'I could go to Zurich and wait for Sutherland to turn up,' Granville said over the telephone, 'but even if I alert you straight away, he may have left by the time you arrive.'

'Then we will both have to go to Zurich and wait for him there,' Spartak replied.

'Is it safe for you to go? I'm just not sure if you are wanted for anything? I've served my time, so I should be okay, but it may be more dangerous for you to travel.'

'He has stolen from me,' Spartak roared. 'No one steals from me and survives. I want my money back and one of you is going to pay.'

'Yes, yes, I understand that,' Granville spluttered. 'I just wondered if it would be better for me to see him, in the first instance?'

'You think you can persuade him better than me?'

'No, of course not. I just thought it might be precarious for you to enter a Western jurisdiction, given the state of the war in Kosovo.'

'Switzerland is a neutral country. No one is going to arrest me,' Spartak reassured him. 'Besides, I need a holiday. I will meet you there.'

The next morning Ian went to work and gave Nick a call.

'I'm working out of London at the moment,' Nick said, 'and I'm hoping you can meet me. I'm afraid it's very important.'

'I need to come to London anyway, but why is it so important?' Ian asked.

'I think your life could be in danger and I need to talk to you. Sorry to be so alarmist.'

Ian was quiet for a few moments and then replied softly: 'Well, given the urgency, I could set off now and meet you for something to eat tonight.'

'Yes, let's do that.'

'Okay, I will call you later with a time and venue after I have booked something.'

Ian stood up to leave looking rather anxious.

'I'm going to London,' he said to Holly. 'Last minute thing.'

Holly looked surprised. 'Oh, but I have just opened the post and the valuation for Horn Beck House has come in. It's £20,000 lower. What do you want me to do?'

Ian took the valuation from her and read it quickly.

'I'll ring Dr Holt from the station,' he replied.

'Too late,' Holly said as Ian gathered a couple of files and put them in his briefcase. 'I've got Rachel Armfield on the phone for you now.'

Ian took the receiver from Holly and spoke to Rachel from reception.

'We've got a copy of the new valuation,' Rachel said. 'What shall we do?'

'I think I should lower your offer by £20,000. I would

do it by sending a letter to the Butlers' solicitors. We could make it more tempting by saying that subject to agreeing the price we are ready to exchange contracts,' Ian replied, rushing out an answer.

'Are we ready to exchange?' Rachel asked.

'We will be by the time they respond. The mortgagee will have to re-issue the mortgage offer but given the amount of equity you will have, that is just a formality.'

'Okay, please go ahead,' Rachel instructed.

'My pleasure,' Ian replied.

'You're going to miss your train,' Holly said, looking concerned.

Ian looked at his watch and hesitated.

'You know what? I'm going to drive. Can you book me into The Ritz and check they can take the car? Oh, and I will need somewhere for dinner. Table for two at about 8 o'clock. I will ring you in a couple of hours when I stop for a break.'

'Yes sir,' Holly said, giving Ian a friendly salute.

Ian opened the throttle of the E-type and headed down the M1, telephoning Holly from a motorway service station after two hours straight driving.

'The Ritz is full, so I've had to book you into a little bed and breakfast on Brook Street,' she said.

'Bed and breakfast! What's it called?' Ian asked, with a tone of exasperation in his voice.

'Claridge's,' Holly replied, laughing as she said it.

'And I've booked you in for dinner at the hotel as well, as it's all last minute.'

'Excellent, thank you Holly.'

'There's more! I've also reserved a table for you in the cocktail bar at 7pm.'

'Ah, is there no limit to your talents!' Ian exclaimed before continuing: 'Can you ring Nick Rowe and let him know the arrangements, and can you also ask Ed to do a letter to the Butlers' solicitors lowering our offer by £20,000 please?'

'I'm on it,' Holly replied.

Four hours and fifteen minutes after setting off, Ian pulled up outside the front entrance to the hotel. A doorman called Craig looked admiringly at the Jag and opened the car door for him.

'Welcome to Claridge's Mr Sutherland. I'll take care of the car for you. How many bags do you have sir?'

'Just the one,' Ian replied, having packed very quickly whilst making arrangements for Sky.

Ian was shown to the reception area and checked in. Claridge's was bigger than The Ritz and had more of a business atmosphere. The clientele was also slightly different – more Americans and more celebrities.

One of the receptionists, Eimear, showed Ian the bar and the dining room, and then took him up in the lift to his bedroom. It was newly refurbished and immaculately clean, and decorated in soft, relaxing colours. It had its own dressing room with a dressing table, full length mirrors and plenty of space for hanging clothes. Ian wished he was staying longer.

As she turned to go, Eimear pointed out a complimentary lemon cake which had been placed on a table near the bedroom window.

'Would you like a glass of champagne to accompany the cake sir?'

Ian was going to head straight into town, but the cake looked too good to leave, so he decided to have a slice instead of lunch.

'A glass of fresh orange would be good, thank you, Eimear – if that's the right pronunciation?'

'Certainly, sir. It's pronounced Emer. It's Irish.'

'Oh, I love all things Irish!' Ian replied, a little flirtatiously.

The cake was delicious. In fact, it was so delicious, Ian had two slices as it had clearly just been made by one of the pastry chefs in the hotel kitchen.

Ten minutes later, Ian was walking up Burlington Arcade, hoping he would be able to fit into his new trousers, as he made his way to Anderson & Sheppard - but the cake was very light, he kept reassuring himself.

As he entered the elegant premises of his tailor all Ian's worries drained away. There was something comforting about the place. The leather sofa in front of the fire place and the mahogany furniture. The customer records and rolls of cloth. It oozed tradition, but most of all, the warm welcome made this one of his favourite destinations in London.

It was easy to choose, for instance, a navy-blue suit for work. You would be offered a few favoured cloths to select from and the tailors would have made similar outfits many times before. This time, however, Ian was collecting something more casual and he was unsure how it would turn out, as there was so much more to think about.

You had to match colour and texture; style and accessories – not things Ian was used to thinking about. However, Danny, the Head Cutter and Master Tailor, had been as helpful as ever and now it was time to see the finished products.

With Danny's help, Ian had chosen an Irish linen mid-navy-blue jacket with turned up cuffs and mottled-brown horn buttons, matched with some half-lined white cotton trousers, to be worn with brown suede loafers from Cleverley's.

Danny took Ian into one of the fitting rooms and he tried everything on. It all fitted perfectly. Danny stood back and admired the outfit with pride.

'I always say clothes should protect, decorate and communicate, and I think these fulfil the brief sir.'

'They certainly do Danny,' Ian responded, as he tried to assimilate this new look. The jacket was brighter than he had imagined and a little lighter in colour, but in the summer heat it would look better than a darker navy.

'Talking of protection sir, I think a Panama would add an important finishing touch.'

'You're right and it will be useful for events such as The Yorkshire Show. Where do you think I should go for that?'

'Oh, there's only one place sir. Lock & Co in St James's.'

'Of course. I should have known,' Ian replied.

Whilst Ian had tried on his new clothes, one of Danny's colleagues had pressed his suit and returned it looking as good as new.

'Thank you,' Ian said, and 'thank you Danny for all your help.' Ian shook Danny's hand and headed for Lock & Co.

Again, there was something reassuring about the premises. The ancient wooden facia almost held together by the thick green and white paint. Inside were two gentlemen in pin-striped suits serving customers – one with a wife directing operations – so Ian stood quietly in the corner looking at the hats and waiting for someone to become free. Just then, a square-bodied American walked through the door and came over to Ian.

'Hey, you got any cashmere baseball caps?' he asked, in a deep Southern drawl.

'I don't work here, I'm a customer,' Ian replied, rather

acidly.

The American stepped back a pace and a female assistant shot out of a room to the rear.

'I'm sorry sir, we don't sell baseball caps,' she said.

The American continued backing towards the exit, moving his head up and down and from side to side as he did so, taking in his surroundings.

'You been here a while huh?'

'Well, actually these are our more modern premises which we moved to in 1759,' she replied. 'Prior to that we were on the other side of the street where we opened in 1676.'

The poor American made a quick departure as the lady turned to assist Ian.

'Priceless,' Ian muttered to himself. 'Absolutely priceless.'

Back at Claridge's, Eimear did a double take when she saw Ian arrive carrying a full-length suit bag and large hat box.

'I said I like all things Irish,' Ian remarked, unzipping the suit bag so she could see his new Irish linen jacket.

'You said love,' Eimear replied, suddenly blushing and looking away to hide her embarrassment. Ian adored her soft, Irish lilt.

'That too,' he said, as he headed for the lift.

There was an ambience of excitement in the bar with

several glamorous women distracting Ian from noticing that Nick Rowe was already sat waiting at one of the tables.

'I hope you haven't been waiting long?' Ian asked, as Nick stood and they shook hands.

'No, I've just arrived,' Nick replied.

A cocktail waiter immediately proffered a menu but Ian hesitated when he saw the huge choice on offer. It would take time to study, which was difficult when you were trying to talk to someone, but to have a simple gin and tonic or a Martini seemed a shame when there was so much else on offer.

'Can you recommend something?' Ian asked the cocktail waiter. 'Nothing too alcoholic and I like citrus flavours. Something dry and sharp.'

'Then I recommend the Corpse Reviver No 2,' the waiter replied, pointing to the appropriate entry on the menu. We mix Plymouth Gin, Lillet Blanc, Combier Triple Sec and lemon juice in a cocktail shaker with ice, add a teaspoon of sugar syrup and a dash of Pernod Absinthe and garnish with an orange coin.'

'Well, I can't argue with that,' Ian conceded.

'I'll have the same,' Nick chimed.

'So, what's this all about?' Ian asked as soon the waiter was out of earshot. 'You seemed pretty concerned on the telephone.'

'I am concerned,' Nick replied. 'I told you I had been

tasked with observing the KLA, firstly in Kosovo and now in the UK. Well, the paramilitary leader I mentioned to you is using a money launderer based in northern Cyprus called Frederick Granville and, I'm sorry to say, we have just recorded a call from him during which he orders a couple of Kosovan KLA members to kill you.'

'They've already tried,' Ian replied.

'Already! What happened?'

'They failed; I'm pleased to say.' Ian wasn't being flippant. He was looking deadly serious.

'I will tell you more over dinner,' he continued, 'but firstly, tell me this. You said 'we.' Who's we?'

'I thought I told you. I've been supporting the NATO operations in Kosovo but, basically, I'm working with the intelligence services monitoring the serious organised crime operations of a paramilitary warlord called Spartak. He is expanding his tobacco smuggling activities into the UK. Apparently, there is much less competition than in Europe where contraband tobacco is more common.'

'I've heard of him,' Ian said. 'Another old adversary of mine called Hayden Boyes spilled the beans.'

Just then the cocktail waiter returned with their drinks and two small bowls containing olives and nuts.

'Unfortunately, you're not out of the woods yet. I understand you are going to Zurich where they intend to take care of you,' Nick said, laying a heavy emphasis on the last part of his sentence.

'How do you know all this?' Ian asked incredulously.

'I told you. We are monitoring Granville's phone calls and Spartak's but he makes less of them. It's funny with Menwith Hill being so close to you.'

'I thought Menwith Hill was American.'

'It's owned by the Ministry of Defence, but made available to the US Department of Defense. The US authorities have administrative control.'

'And they monitor peoples phone calls?'

'GCHQ are in there. They provide intelligence support for the US, the UK and certain other allies whose interests are aligned.'

'But how can they do it? How do they know it is Granville making the call and how do they know when he is making it?'

'The power of the network is astounding,' Nick replied. 'It's the largest electronic monitoring station in the world.' He grabbed a handful of nuts and spread out a napkin which had been provided by the cocktail waiter. 'I will spell the codename for you. Do not say it out loud.'

Nick arranged the nuts on the napkin to spell out the letters: ECH. 'Remember those,' he said. Then he did the same again with the letters EL and finally he did it a third time with the letters ON.

Ian nodded to indicate he understood. The codename was ECHELON.

'It's a global spying network that can eavesdrop on

every single phone call, fax or email anywhere on the planet. It works by voice recognition and homes in on key words and phrases.'

The cocktail waiter saw the nuts in a pile on the napkin and came over.

'Is everything all right?' he asked.

Nick tipped the nuts into his hand and scooped them into his mouth.

'Fine, thank you,' Ian replied, 'but we will have another round please.'

'Certainly sir. The same again?'

'Yes please. That just hit the spot.'

Ian and Nick looked at each other without saying anything whilst the waiter tidied the table and went about his business. Eventually, Ian broke the silence.

'So, do you think Granville will have a second go?'

Nick sat back and sipped some of his cocktail to moisten his mouth after eating the nuts.

'We picked up early on that Granville has some sort of vendetta against you and it was Granville that issued the kill order, but this show is being driven by Spartak. It's his money you've blown.'

'Spartak's?'

'Yes.'

'I didn't realise that.'

'That's why it's so serious. I don't think he will take it lying down.'

The second Corpse Reviver No 2 arrived and Ian raised his glass in salute to Nick.

'Cheers,' he said. 'I think I might be in need of my corpse reviving from what you are telling me!'

'I can't help you there but I do have an idea of how I can help you.'

'How?' Ian replied.

'Let me go to Zurich for you.'

Ian stared across the bar and contemplated Nick's offer for a moment. For once, he chose the more cautious option.

'That's not a bad idea actually. I would just need you to go to Granville's Bank and find out how much is held in a numbered account belonging to one of my clients and then report back to me. I could pay your expenses because the client would have to pay mine anyway.'

'Consider it done,' Nick replied, just as a waiter approached with a tray to say their table was ready in the dining room and he would carry their drinks through.

They made their way across the bar and as they reached the door into the hotel lobby, Ian put his arm on Nick's shoulder to allow him to go first.

'It's very good of you to do this for me,' Ian said.

'No problem. What are friends for?' Nick replied.

It was a kind act of friendship but neither of them had thought things through. They were only kicking the can down the road.

Chapter Sixteen

It was good to be back in the office. There was something reassuring about the routine and Ian just wanted to be able to sit down quietly and get on with some work, free from the rush of travelling and the pressure of meetings.

Holly and Ed were sat at their desks, Sky was curled up in the corner and Rita had popped into the town centre to get them all some fresh coffee - Ian's treat.

Ian didn't have to go to Zurich, Granit and Valon were not in the country and whatever Granville's intentions, he lacked the ability to execute them, so Ian was feeling better about things. Spartak was, perhaps, more of a worry, but he was a paramilitary leader in a war zone. It all seemed too distant to be of immediate concern.

'Yes, it's going to be a good day,' Ian said out loud to anyone that was listening, which at that precise moment was probably only Sky and she didn't seem very interested.

The telephone rang and Holly put the Butlers' solicitor through to Ian. He complained bitterly that there was no real issue and said that, in any case, the farmer was not bothered about the situation. He was clearly regurgitating his clients' instructions and they were probably going to check that he had done so, therefore, Ian simply listened politely. However, after beating around the bush, he said his clients would reluctantly accept the reduced offer, provided exchange of contracts took place by the end of the week.

Victory! Ian tried the various numbers and it was Rachel who first picked up the telephone. He gave her the good news.

'Oh, that's wonderful! Thank you so much. I can't believe it; you've just saved us twenty thousand pounds!'

'My pleasure. Now, all we need to do is wait until after completion and see if we can come to a more formal arrangement with the farmer.'

'Do we need to come to see you before we can exchange? To give you a deposit and sign the contract?' Rachel asked with a hint of anxiety.

'Yes please,' Ian replied.

'It's just that I have a breast reconstruction scheduled every day for the rest of this week. I'm not sure how I am going to find the time.'

'Dr Holt can sign the contract on your behalf,' Ian suggested. 'You will need to sign the mortgage deed and transfer deed personally, but they don't need signing until just before completion.'

'Really? Oh, that's wonderful. Thank you so much. That's a huge help.' Rachel paused momentarily. 'Tell me what do you like to drink because Tony will most certainly want to bring you something.'

'Oh, there's no need for that, but may I ask you something?' Ian said hesitantly.

'Fire away,' Rachel replied.

'Are you a plastic surgeon by any chance?'

'Yes.'

'I was wondering,' Ian said still treading carefully, 'when I introduced you to Rita, did you notice the scar on her face?'

'Yes, I did. From its width and indentation, I would say it was left to heal without any medical intervention and from its pink colour I would say it happened less than six months ago.'

'Wow, you do know your stuff! Is there anything that can be done about it?'

'Yes. We could re-open the wound and re-suture it with fine stitches to make a thin and non-indented scar. The wound would need deep stitches that remain and then a superficial continuous stitch that is removed. Initially, the scar would remain pink, but it would settle down quickly and we could use some silicone scar ointment to help with that.'

'So, I think you are saying you would cut out the existing scar and after healing Rita would be left with just a thin line. Is that right?'

'Basically, yes. I would tell her that I can't get rid of the scar, but I can certainly improve it.'

Ian took a deep breath and continued:

'Rita's from Kosovo. She and her family recently claimed asylum in the UK, but she was brutally attacked by a member of the Kosovan Liberation Army as she attempted to escape. He slashed her face with a Stanley knife. She's only sixteen and she has her whole life in front of her. I'd be really grateful if you could help her?'

Rachel could sense the earnest desperation in Ian's voice to restore some balance of fair play.

'It would be my privilege,' she replied emphatically. 'Get her to register with Tony as her GP and I'll make sure he refers her to me.'

'Thank you,' Ian replied, with a genuine relief. 'Oh, and by the way. I don't want her to know I've said anything. I'll ask Holly to suggest a visit to the doctor's and perhaps you and Tony could take it from there?'

'Of course,' Rachel promised.

Perhaps another reason for Ian's high spirits was his excitement about his intended date with Inga on Saturday night. He parked the E-type outside the cafeteria and walked around the front to the back door. This time he knocked on it more gently.

'Come in,' Inga shouted from upstairs.

Ian opened the door into the small kitchen which had been carved out of the ground floor of the café.

'I'm upstairs,' Inga called when she heard him enter.

The stairs were straight in front of him and Ian made his way up slowly just in case this was not what she was expecting. Inga stuck her head around a bedroom door and leant sideways to look down the stairs which looked cool with her long blonde hair falling towards the ground.

'Make yourself comfortable in the sitting room. I won't be long,' she said.

There was a bathroom on the left at the top of the stairs and then a small bedroom. The bedroom seemed cluttered, but Ian noticed a squat rack with a bar and weights resting at shoulder height. The weights looked heavy.

Ian turned to his right where there were two further rooms overlooking the front – Inga's bedroom and the sitting room. He continued into the sitting room and sat down on a sofa that was angled towards a television in the corner. The carpet was cheap and poorly fitted – in fact it looked as though there was no underlay. However, Ian realised that this was tied accommodation for a temporary worker, so it would be surprising if the fittings were anything other than basic.

Immediately, Ian noticed a raven in the opposite corner to the television and it gave him a bit of a surprise although he realised it was stuffed. It was perched on the branch of an artificial tree, set in a pot. It was very artistic and very realistic, even if somewhat sinister.

He had forgotten how large they were – much bigger than the common crow, but then he remembered he had seen some real ones at the Tower of London a few years ago. He was trying to recall the myth. Something about England would not fall to a foreign invader so long as there were ravens at the Tower.

He decided to ask Inga about the raven. He thought it would make a good icebreaker, but then she appeared at the sitting room doorway and his mind went blank.

He noticed her face first – the blush rose lipstick and smoky eyes with winged eyeliner, matching so perfectly her ice-blonde hair. But then he noticed her outfit – a tight black corset accentuating her waist and skinny black jeans with a dark grey denim shirt tied loosely at the waist. She looked tall and he saw she was wearing knee-high, black leather boots with a two-and-a-half-inch block heel – much more to his liking than the biker boots she had worn the last time he saw her.

'Wow. You look fantastic,' he said, immediately standing up to greet her.

'Thank you. I thought you would prefer this to the goth look,' she replied.

'Are you a goth?' Ian asked. It was a clumsy question, but he was rather naïve in these matters and, she seemed to welcome the opportunity to answer.

'According to the aficionados I'm not goth enough! It's quite challenging trying to channel an alt lifestyle whilst looking like a balanced adult. I can't wear strong make-up and lots of accessories at work and the blonde hair doesn't help.'

'Well, I think you look great!' Ian replied.

He held open his right arm to allow Inga to go ahead and they walked back along the landing not quite abreast of each other. In the confinement of that space, he could sense her presence. She was taller than any other girlfriend he had known and she had a powerful physique. As they passed the bedroom with the squat rack and weights, Ian noticed again the large size of the rubber bumper plates.

'Can you actually lift that?' he asked.

Inga peeled away from him and positioned herself under the bar, resting it on the back of her shoulders. She straightened her legs slightly so that she was bearing the weight and then dropped into the squat position. In gym gear she would have looked good. In skinny jeans and boots, she looked amazing!

Inga straightened up and released the bar back onto the squat rack.

'Any more questions?' she asked, triumphantly.

'Impressive!' Ian replied. 'How much does that weigh?'

'70kg. I'm five foot nine and weigh exactly 11 stone, so I can lift my own body weight.'

They walked down the stairs and across the front garden to where the E-type was waiting and Ian opened the door for her.

'Are you okay with the top down?' he asked, concerned

that she might be worried what the wind would do to her hair.

'I wouldn't have it any other way,' she replied, giving him a lovely smile.

It was a beautiful drive to the village of East Witton, with the sun shining on the Yorkshire dales and Inga's hair blowing in all different directions. Ian liked it when she brushed it out of her face with her fingers, her grey chrome-like nail varnish complementing the aluminium console of the Jaguar.

He drove sensibly but hugged the corners and, as he did so, Inga would occasionally place her hand on his thigh to counter balance the gravitational forces, which he liked.

'I love these country roads,' he said, smiling at her.

The Blue Lion was a traditional country pub with wooden tables and chairs and a log fire which formed a central feature even when not lit in the summer. It did, however, have a more upmarket clientele than the average public house, as it was renowned for its well-stocked bar and the quality of its food.

The Twice Baked Wensleydale Cheese Soufflé with Chive Cream Sauce was, ostensibly, the raison d'être for their visit so they both had to order that and they continued copying each other by asking for the Grilled Fillet of Halibut with New Potatoes, Buttered Spinach and Hollandaise Sauce to follow.

Ian ordered a bottle of Meursault, hoping the Chardonnay grape would stand up to the sauces, but limited himself to one glass as he was driving.

The whole meal was exquisite. The tang of the cheese soufflé, the way the fish flaked at the touch of the knife and the honied depth of flavour in the wine all made for a perfect meal.

Spinach wouldn't have been Ian's first choice of vegetable, but it got him back on to the topic of the weights.

'So, given your weight lifting abilities, you must be into fitness?' Ian asked.

'No,' Inga replied, laughing. 'I'm interested in dark fashion and vintage glamour. I lift weights so I can fit into my corsets. Squat lifts are not just good for your quads and glutes - they strengthen your core as well.'

'Well, I'm all for corsets,' Ian joked as he looked at her narrow waist and accentuated breasts.

'I love them! I have a 28-inch waist and I can close a 24-inch corset so that's a 4-inch reduction.'

Ian looked puzzled.

'Isn't that bad for you?' he asked.

'You have to train your body slowly and adjust to a more upright position, gradually achieving higher reductions at a comfortable pace. The most difficult part was to get used to sitting upright for long periods of time and my muscles used to ache terribly, but that passed eventually, and now my posture is more upright even without wearing a corset. Recently, I have been able to hang out in this completely closed 24-inch corset for a whole day!'

Ian simply raised his eyebrows not knowing what to say. He had no knowledge of such subjects, but Inga obviously favoured the traditionally styled corset with synthetic whalebone, rather than the more common basque underwear usually worn as lingerie. He thought it must be uncomfortable.

'There's something I want to ask you,' she said, changing the subject.

Ian gulped wondering what was coming next.

Inga put her hand into the breast pocket of her shirt and pulled out a folded piece of paper that had been torn out of a glossy magazine. She flattened it out on the table and turned it towards Ian so that he could read it.

It was an advert for a dinner dance at Le Grand Hotel in Paris on the 21st August to celebrate the 55th anniversary of its liberation. It said guests had to wear period dress.

'Looks interesting,' Ian said. 'A lot of my clients were involved in the Second World War because that generation has just reached the age when they start thinking about their wills so, naturally, I've become interested in it too.'

'And I love Paris and the post-war fashion. Seamed stockings and all that sort of thing. People just wanted fun after all the hardship and I can relate to that. I really want to go and was going to ask my mother, but that would be boring, so I wondered if you would come with me?' She paused for a moment and then continued: 'I would pay my own way, obviously, because we would need two hotel bedrooms.'

'Well, I'm not going as an American GI.'

'So you'll come? You could go as a member of the French Resistance.'

'I'll think about it. Let me check my diary,' Ian replied.

'Okay. It would be exciting though,' she persisted, making her eyes open wide.

'Actually, I do know a little hotel in the Latin quarter. I'll ring them on Monday to see if they have any rooms because it's only a couple of weeks away.'

Just then a waitress came over and asked if they would like dessert.

'I couldn't. I think I'm going to burst!' Inga replied.

'Coffee?'

Ian looked at Inga questioningly.

'Espresso please,' she said.

They chatted about France for a while as they sipped their coffees and Inga finished her wine and then they made their way back to the carpark.

Inga was slightly tipsy and leaning on Ian for support. In the low-slung seat of the E-type, however, she was clearly uncomfortable.

'Oh, I'm so full,' she said as she leant forward and put her arm up the back of her shirt to loosen the laces on her corset. It had pin and hook fasteners at the front and as she sank back into the seat, Ian noticed that the top one had popped open, temptingly revealing a little more than she probably realised.

Inga rambled a bit on the way home, mainly about Paris, and Ian listened whilst letting his own thoughts drift to matters that concerned him. He wasn't sure about Inga. There were things she said that he found disturbing and other things that concerned him. She was different from anyone he had ever dated before, but then he would look at her and forget all of that. She was just so attractive.

He stopped the Jag outside the café and was about to get out, to open the door for her, but somehow, they automatically leant towards each other and started kissing. Ian placed his hand on Inga's waist and felt the stiffness of the corset. There was something erotic about that. She started unbuttoning his shirt as he moved his hand up towards her left breast. He slid his hand under the top of her corset and cradled her breast. Like a piece of forbidden fruit, it felt so good.

They continued kissing as Inga ran her hand around his sculptured chest. It felt so warm as she pressed firmly against his torso, as though she was grading a lamb for slaughter. Ian moved his hand down again towards the button on her jeans but, as soon as he tried to undo it, she pushed his hand away.

'I've got to go now,' she said, giving him a full stop of

a kiss before getting out of the car. 'See you soon.'

'See you soon,' he sighed.

Granville was distraught. He had barely slept, but he had nowhere to run – nowhere that Spartak wouldn't find him. He had no choice but to give Spartak the bad news.

He called in at his bank, checked out an idea that came to him in the middle of the night and walked the short distance to the Baur Au Lac hotel, set in private parkland on the northern edge of Lake Zurich.

Spartak was in a surprisingly good mood, taking breakfast on the private rooftop terrace with his wife and two daughters. Polina was in the background. The girls were typical teenagers but, for security reasons, he kept a tight rein on them.

By Western standards, this was probably the first proper holiday they had ever experienced. Staying in one of the best hotels in Switzerland, set in private gardens near the lake with old world luxury, fabulous food, and sunshine, was having a calming effect on Spartak. He was feeling magnanimous. Nevertheless, there would be no small talk. This was business.

When he saw Granville approach, he stood up, wiped his mouth with his napkin and indicated they should look at the view from a corner of the terrace.

'I have some good news and some not so good news,' Granville said, trying to put a positive spin on things.

'Give me the bad news,' Spartak replied, picking his teeth with his little finger.

'Sutherland sent someone to the bank yesterday on his behalf, so I don't think he is coming to Zurich.'

Spartak took a deep breath and shook his head in dismay.

'And the good news?'

'I've looked at the account he's accessed. It contains £300,000.'

'Well, transfer it to me,' Spartak said, raising his hands upwards to signify the solution was obvious.

'It's not that simple. We need a password to complete a transfer and we don't know it.'

Spartak slapped his forehead with the palm of his hand.

'I gave you two weeks to sort this and you have had about four. I take it that the completion date has passed?'

'Yes.'

'So, you have lost my money and I warned you what would happen?'

'Yes.'

Just then Spartak's younger daughter ran up to him.

'Daddy they've brought your French toast with fresh berries.'

'One moment, my sweet,' Spartak said, smiling at her and turning her gently back towards the table with the palm of his hand. Then he whispered in Granville's ear: 'Two weeks. In two weeks, you will have the password and have transferred the money to me or arranged a meeting for me to extract the password from him.' He waved his index finger in Granville's face. 'I will not let this deadline pass. In two weeks, I will have my money or I will pin my calling card on your chest.'

'Hi Holly,' Nick said as he bounded into the office. 'Ian about?'

'I'll just get him,' Holly replied, giving him a broad smile.

'Nick!' Ian shouted, clasping Nick's hand. 'How did you get on?'

'Got the info. The account has £300,000 in it.'

Ian nodded several times.

'And all undeclared; but not for long. Look, I'm very grateful for all your help.'

'No problem, my friend but from here you're on your own, so tread carefully.'

'What do you mean?'

'I've been sent back to Northern Ireland. Just collecting my kit and then heading out tomorrow.'

'I thought that was all sorted now, following the Good Friday agreement?'

'Apparently, there are still some people who need persuading,' Nick said, giving Ian a wink.

Ian laughed. Somehow, he didn't think Nick would be debating the merits of his case across a negotiating table.

Simon Black was also smiling to himself as he enjoyed the evening sun, leisurely walking home along Chelsea Embankment. Nick Rowe had allowed friendship to cloud his judgement. That's why he had reported he was superfluous to the operation. Now his plan was one step nearer coming to fruition. Of course, there would be risk but you must look at things objectively, he reassured himself. He muttered something under his breath. A woman with a baby in a pushchair walking in the opposite direction paused for a second, thinking he had spoken to her, but he hadn't even seen her so she carried on with his words ringing in her ears:

'I always get my own way in the end,' he had said, before repeating: 'I always get my own way in the end.'

Chapter Seventeen

Ian had packed and it was time to collect Inga, but he called into the office first for one final check before they departed for Paris.

All was well, except the Inland Revenue had written in response to Ian's declaration that Graham Towers had £300,000 in a Swiss bank account. He picked up the telephone to Kath.

'I've heard back from the Revenue and I'm afraid you won't have much change left after the income tax, interest and penalties,' he said.

'Go on. How much do they want?' she asked.

'£285,000. They're asking for 95%!'

'Well, it's to be expected, I suppose,' she said letting out a long sigh. 'To be honest, I still don't think we've done too badly if you take into account everything else that has gone on over the years. If we pay, will they unfreeze the estate?'

'Yes, upon payment they will, but not before.'

'Well go ahead as soon as possible please Ian.'

'I will. I've just got to work out the best way of doing it, logistically, that is.'

Job done, Ian left final instructions with Ed and Holly to cries of: 'Just go,' and shot up to the cafeteria by the entrance to Fountains Abbey. He knocked on the door to the flat, and, once again, Inga shouted down the stairs asking him to wait in the sitting room.

This time, Ian didn't sit, but paced up and down looking at his watch.

'We've got to get going,' he shouted across the landing, worried that they might miss their flight.

'I won't be long,' Inga replied.

Ian turned back into the sitting room and noticed the raven staring at him ominously.

'What do you want?' he said crossly.

'Excuse me?' Inga replied, as she appeared in the doorway.

'Oh, I'm sorry,' Ian said laughing. 'I was just talking to the raven! How come you have a raven in your sitting room?'

'I like taxidermy. It's a way of keeping alive those things that are dead. In Sweden, ravens are known as the ghosts of murdered people and he reminds me of someone.'

'Sounds a bit weird to me,' Ian mumbled under his breath.

'Not if you dream about living in a Gothic castle surrounded by woods! Ravens are very clever birds. They have been observed calling wolves to the site of dead animals. The wolves tear apart the carcass, leaving the scraps more accessible to the birds.'

'Okay, well on that cheery note, let's catch that plane, shall we?' Ian asked sarcastically.

'I don't know what you're being so stuffy about. You're the one that was talking to it,' Inga replied, gently teasing him.

Amazingly, they were on time and the flight was on time although as they approached Charles de Gaulle airport there was some air turbulence causing the aeroplane to behave more like a rollercoaster during its descent. Ian had been keeping quiet about a migrainous headache, but now he also felt sick. The red-light instructing passengers to, 'fasten your seatbelts,' had just come on when Ian stood up and made haste towards the toilet. A male flight attendant blocked his way and said: 'non' only to stand quickly aside when he realised what was about to happen. Inga was watching and thought it was hilarious. Luckily Ian made it just in time although all the other passengers heard what followed and gave Ian a wide berth when they disembarked.

The vomiting eased the pain in his head, but Ian was pale and relieved to see a chauffeur was waiting for them, as arranged, when they exited the airport. He took their luggage and escorted them to a black S-Class Mercedes with light grey leather seats. Ian sat back and poured a glass of Evian as they started the journey to the hotel.

They passed all the usual sites such as the Arc de Triomphe and the Place de la Concorde, Inga looking out of the windows and occasionally leaning across Ian to see what could be seen from his side. Eventually, they cruised alongside the Jardin des Tuileries and crossed the Seine via Pont Neuf before following the one-way system into Rue Christine.

Inga was taken aback. One minute they were travelling along multi-laned roadways congested with traffic and as soon as they had crossed the bridge, they were crawling up Rue Christine which was barely wide enough for the Mercedes to pass. It stopped beside an archway, opposite a cinema and the chauffeur said:

'Nous sommes ici.'

Inga gave Ian a questioning glance, but before he could say anything, a doorman appeared and opened the car door for her, whilst a second doorman arrived with a trolley and asked the chauffeur how many bags were in the boot.

The doormen guided them through the archway into a private courtyard and then up some steps into the grand entrance of Relais Christine, an elegant boutique hotel, where a receptionist called Marie, welcomed them and the doormen prepared to deliver their luggage to the appropriate rooms.

Marie showed them Inga's room first, which was just so stylish. Perfumed and spotlessly clean, the walls were decorated with exquisite wallpaper, the bed was adorned with pillows and cushions and the bathroom had gleaming tiles and gold fittings together with all the toiletries you could wish for.

Ian agreed to meet Inga downstairs in an hour and then Marie showed Ian to his room which was equally pleasing.

Just beyond reception were the lounges, one a few steps lower down than the other, but both comfortable, cosy and beautifully decorated and furnished. Ian sat in a huge armchair waiting for Inga, closed his eyes and relaxed. There was something special about this hotel – perhaps the fact that it was small made it more homely. That was it. The staff were friendly, every comfort was catered for and Ian felt completely at home.

Inga came down the stairs wearing a shell pink, V-necked, fitted, ribbed dress which fell below the knee, had short sleeves and large horn-coloured buttons up the front. Ian stood up to greet her.

'I'm wearing these because you said we had a long way to walk,' Inga said, lifting and wiggling her right foot to show off her white trainers with a Nike logo in pink.

'Perfect,' Ian replied.

It wasn't too far. They went back over Pont Neuf, stopping half way across to take some photographs as the sun set over the Seine and then they walked beside the river along Quai du Louvre, through Jardin des

Tuileries to Place Vendôme. Inga stared in wonder at the magnificence of the square with the splendid hotels, built under Louis XIV in the classical French style, forming the boundaries and Napoleon's column at its centre. The feeling of spaciousness added to its grandeur.

From there it was only a short walk up Rue de la Paix to Café de la Paix situate at the junction of Boulevard des Capucines and Place de l'Opera.

Ian had booked dinner at Café de la Paix because it was on the ground floor of Le Grand Hotel and he wanted to get his bearings for the dinner dance the following evening. It was also a famous meeting spot, a central hub in Paris, and the perfect place to watch the world go by.

Luckily, they got a window seat, but choosing from the menu was not completely straightforward mainly owing to Ian's aversion to unconventional food. He massively admired French culinary skills but if an item on the menu included the word *tartare*, Ian wouldn't touch it and certain iconic dishes such as *Escargots* were completely off his radar. Ian's view was that they were first eaten during a time of national poverty and dressed up in parsley butter to make them palatable. Whoever managed to turn them into a delicacy deserved a medal for marketing.

Consequently, Ian ordered another signature dish, namely Soupe à' L'oignon Gratinee but he felt he was being predictable. Inga ordered the Foie Gras and to follow they both ordered the sea bass which wasn't particularly French.

'So, how do you like my Barbie look?' Inga asked, taking Ian off guard.

'You always look nice,' he replied.

'Oh, very diplomatic. But seriously, which me do you prefer?'

'I like whichever is the real you. I've nothing against alt fashion – I thought you looked fantastic in the mauve make-up the first time you came to the cottage – but you are naturally beautiful so you look good in whatever you wear.'

'Thank you,' Inga replied, blushing not just facially, but also around the base of her neck.

Ian should have probably left it there but if you are interested in people, it is hard not to ask questions.

'Anyway, what drew you to dark fashion in the first place? Why are you so interested in it?'

Inga stared into her wine glass and looked a little sad.

'Sorry,' Ian said. 'There is no need to answer that.'

'No, it's okay,' she replied, relaxing a little. 'It is a mask; a sort of defence. I felt socially insecure and the dark make-up was a way of getting noticed.'

'So, you want to be noticed when you dress like that?'

'Yes. It's an aggressive response. A way of showing strength, but that worried me. I don't want to be like my father.'

'I'm sure you're nothing like him,' Ian replied, getting

a little out of his depth.

'You don't even know him, but I've toned things down since I was a teenager. I'm not nearly as alt as I used to be! I still have a fascination with,' Inga paused and didn't finish her sentence.

'What?' Ian asked automatically.

'The dark side,' Inga replied in a funny voice trying to lighten the mood. 'Anyway, that brings me to another matter. He's just telephoned me and said he is coming to Paris. He wants us to meet him.'

'How does he know we are here? I thought you were estranged.'

'We are estranged but he said Mum told him. Apparently, he telephones her from time to time to check I am okay.'

'Do you want to meet him?'

'Well, the divorce was almost ten years ago now. I feel I ought to forgive him and move on, but I don't really want to and then again, I do. Sorry, I'm not making any sense. I don't like him and I can't forget what he did to us but he is still my father. Part of me wants to have a relationship with him, but then I remember what he did. I can't explain.'

Ian reached across the table and held her hand.

'You just have. I understand and if you want to meet him, I'm happy to come along.'

'Thank you,' Inga said quietly. 'I will think about it

and telephone him tomorrow.'

After dinner, they walked back to the hotel via a slightly different route, taking Avenue de l'Opera and Rue de Rivoli to Pont Neuf. Ian was in a reflective mood, probably the enervating effect of the sultry August weather. Then it suddenly dawned on him that the Rivoli Bar at the Ritz in London must have been named after or have something to do with Rue de Rivoli – after all, César Ritz opened his eponymous Paris hotel just up the road in Place Vendôme – so he shared his theory with Inga, but her mind was elsewhere.

'Night cap?' Ian asked as they arrived back at Relais Christine.

'Go on then,' Inga replied.

They went into the top lounge where you could help yourself to drinks and write down what you had chosen on an honesty pad. Inga went straight for a peach schnapps but Ian lingered, struggling to decide.

'Can I get you something?' a night porter asked.

'What I would really like is a decaffeinated coffee,' Ian responded, trying to keep his headache at bay.

'No problem, sir. I will make one for you.'

They snuggled down in the sumptuous armchairs, opposite each other, and Inga chatted about fashion and the revival of vintage glamour following the deprivations of war and the liberation of Paris.

'That's why I'm looking forward to tomorrow's dinner

dance so much,' she said.

'What are you wearing?' Ian asked.

'Ah, you will have to wait and see,' she teased.

They stayed up late, talking. Ian wasn't in the mood to get amorous. He was drained by the migraine so he just listened until Inga ran out of steam. She was a little surprised he didn't make a move on her but maybe he preferred black? Eventually, they retired to their own beds. He slept like a log whilst she lay awake anxious about how much she had revealed and wondering whether she should tell him anymore of the gory details.

The next morning, they had breakfast in the lower lounge and agreed to go their separate ways for a morning of shopping. Inga scoured the shops along Champs-Elysées and Ian went to Charvet on the corner of Place Vendôme to find the accessories for his French Resistance outfit.

He realised that the purpose of his outfit was to act as a foil for hers. Inga should be the centre of attention; he should be an appropriate prop, so he had kept things simple. Baggy, clerical grey trousers, the sort Roly Pound would have worn, with a light blue, brushed cotton shirt and a blue, heavy cotton, military-style jacket. To make it French, he bought a beret and a red neckerchief with white spots – hence the trip to Charvet.

They met for lunch at Ladurée on Champs-Elysées, which is something all tourists in Paris ought to do.

Sat outside, at the front, under a green framed portico camouflaged with an abundance of pink roses, they each ordered a club sandwich as a prelude to the world-famous macarons.

'Shall we go to this?' Inga asked, passing Ian another advert she had secreted in her bag.

'Edvard Munch exhibition at the Musée d'Orsay,' Ian said, reading it out aloud. 'Well, we could do. It's actually on the way back to the hotel. I don't know much about art though.'

'You don't need to. The trick is to go and see just one painting or one group of paintings. Those people who say: *I've done the Louvre*, are just idiots.'

'So, have you got one painting you want to see? All I know about him is he painted *The Scream*.'

The waitress appeared at this point with a raspberry macaron for each of them and two cappuccinos.

'Now I can see why this place is famous!' Ian enthused, for it was not just the two outer shells of the macaron which were raspberry flavoured. They sandwiched fresh raspberries which sat on a raspberry fondant and were embellished with a dark chocolate disc on the top which said *Ladurée*.

'There is one I want to see, but you will have to wait until we get there,' Inga said, replying to his earlier question.

The Musée d'Orsay was a grand building which

had been a railway station. So much about Paris was impressive that Ian could only admire the French tenacity to be the best and he had to admit that in architecture and many other aspects, they seemed to have achieved it.

'Here we are,' Inga said triumphantly, standing in front of a painting and hiding the description. 'Tell me what you see.'

The painting depicted the top half of a seated man, dressed in dark grey clothes, with his head bowed and his left arm wrapped around the waist of a woman who was standing over him. She had long, red hair and was embracing him, with her right arm resting on top of his left and her face pressed against his neck. The background was dark with flashes of red.

'It's hard to say. On the one hand, the man seems upset and the woman could simply be comforting him; but, on the other hand, you can't see her mouth. It almost looks as though she is biting the back of his neck and her red hair is falling in strands down his face a bit like streaks of blood.'

Inga clapped her hands in glee.

'Well done! Munch titled this painting *Love and Pain* but later it became known as *Vampire*.

'And you like this sort of thing?'

'The whole exhibition is about the *femme fatale*. It's interesting.'

'It's certainly thought provoking, but if I was hanging something on my wall, I would much prefer a Pissarro.'

'That's the difference between you and me. You hanker for the Garden of Eden. I live in the real world.'

'Aspire; I think is the word,' Ian said after pausing for a moment. 'I aspire for something better. I won't accept the status quo. If we all shine a light, there will be no darkness.'

Inga interlocked her arm with his and dragged him towards the exit and back towards the hotel. She liked challenging him and testing his boundaries. She liked the idea of being a *femme fatale*. For her, love and pain had always gone together. She had never enjoyed one without suffering the other. They were two sides of the same coin that featured in every drama.

If Ian had any reservations, which he did, they vanished when Inga met him in the hotel foyer to go to the dinner dance.

From the front, her outfit was what you would expect. A black, fitted dress falling just below the knee with a boat neck and three-quarter length sleeves. When she turned round, however, it was a different story.

The dress had a V-necked back with large red, satin covered buttons which ran along the right-hand side of the neckline, down the centre of the dress and then off to the right again because the hem of the dress incorporated a lace, pleated fan tail. She wore this with seamed black stockings and Christian Louboutin black patent leather heels with the signature red sole.

Ian knew that her hourglass shape meant she was wearing a corset underneath, hence he had only one thing on his mind – a burning desire to undo the red buttons.

The dinner dance was not quite what they expected although, if they had thought about it, it was as they should have expected.

Most of the guests were elderly and some had fought in the War or were involved in the liberation of Paris. For many it was a reunion, a time to reminisce and they had booked tables with friends. Ian and Inga were, therefore, seated at a table where there were a couple of spare places. They were sat with strangers much older than themselves. People who didn't speak much English, or didn't want to, but who nevertheless were curious about their presence.

'You are Resistance?' an old man kept asking Ian.

'No, I'm just dressed like this out of respect,' Ian replied, feeling slightly intimidated.

Then the old man would say something about the Resistance like: 'there were collaborators.' He would then try to tell a story about collaborators, which Ian would have found quite interesting, if he could understand him better, and if the old man's manner wasn't quite so confrontational. Then he would ask him again: 'You are Resistance?'

All this took place against a background of boeuf bourguignon which Ian thought he would like, but it had an unusually strong flavour, which Inga suggested was because it was made with beef cheeks or perhaps it was just the stock.

Regardless of the reason and the dessert still to follow, as soon as the live band changed from playing jazz music to something you could dance a waltz to, Ian gave Inga the eye and they made their way to the dance floor.

'I'm sorry to have ignored you, but I couldn't get away from the old guy next to me,' Ian said apologetically. 'I think he might be mad!'

'Same,' Inga replied. 'His wife asked me if I could ride a bike!'

Ian could just about manage a waltz but it wasn't really his thing. He wanted Inga to enjoy herself though, so he muddled through a couple of songs until the tempo changed again to a slow dance. They smooched, a little closer now, and Ian felt a button on the back of Inga's dress.

'I need to undo these,' he whispered in her ear.

'Come on then,' she replied grabbing his hand and tugging him in the direction of the exit.

Ian hailed a taxi and they were silent at first with anticipation. Then Ian made some nervous remarks about the other guests at the dinner dance and Inga agreed.

Ian quickly paid the taxi, not waiting for change, and they ran up the steps of Relais Christine hand in hand.

'Nightcap?' the night porter asked as they entered the foyer and he handed them their keys.

'No thank you,' they sang in unison as they bolted up the stairs.

Inga opened her door and Ian followed. She turned and they immediately started kissing as she backed towards the bed. Then, almost as though she was obeying an earlier order, she broke away and presented her back to Ian.

Slowly, he undid the buttons, one by one, and then putting his hands on her shoulders, he pushed apart the dress. It slipped to the floor in a heap around her ankles, revealing the tight black corset underneath.

Inga stepped out of her dress and bent down to remove her shoes.

'No. Keep them on,' he said.

'She did as he asked, and moved cat-like on to the bed, kneeling on it, supporting her upper body with her arms.

Her shape was amazing, irresistible, and within seconds Ian had torn off his clothes.

He held her by the waist and there in the humid heat of a Parisian summer with the sound of traffic and ambulance sirens sounding in the distance, he gave her his all.

Sometimes, love making can be gentle. This was anything but, as Ian, gripped by passion, pounded the depths of her inner most being. Inga groaned with ecstasy only for Ian to pause, to keep control, whilst Inga begged him not to stop.

So continue he did, until, eventually, both satiated, Inga fell on her tummy and Ian dropped down beside her.

He rested for just a minute as she uttered short phrases and continued moaning with delight. Then, brushing aside her hair, he started kissing the back of her neck. She lifted her head slightly and Ian put his hand on her shoulder and rolled her on to her back.

Again, he started tidying her hair which was wet with sweat when he saw something on her left shoulder. It was a tattoo. He had never seen it before. In the dim light of night, it looked like an animal, about the size of a tennis ball. A thick bushy tail wrapped around its base like a bagel with its head and shoulders poking out. It was staring at him in the face.

'What's this?' Ian asked in surprise as he ran his fingers across it.

'That's my fox,' she replied.

Chapter Eighteen

Ian rose early without waking Inga, went back to his room, showered, and put on his running kit. Then he went downstairs to the hotel reception where Marie was already on duty.

'Gosh, you work long hours,' Ian said sympathetically.

'Seven days in a row,' she replied, 'but now I have three days off.'

Ian pulled a little brochure from its display holder, and pointed to the relevant section regarding the hotel spa.

'Can I book a sports massage for about an hour's time?'

'Let me look,' Marie replied, checking the availability. '10am? It is a bit longer.'

'Would it be possible to have two? One for my girlfriend as well?'

'I will check. Yes, we can do this,' she said, after a slight pause.

'That's fine and sorry to ask so many questions, but could you arrange for a dozen red roses to be sent to my girlfriend's room please?'

'This is not a problem,' Marie replied, giving Ian a knowing smile. 'You want to write a card?'

'Yes, please.'

Marie slid a card across the desk to Ian and he wrote a quick message: *Loved last night. See you in the Spa for a massage at 10am or, if you prefer, in the foyer at noon before we meet your father for lunch. Love, Ian.*

Business dealt with, Ian could now go on a run to clear his head. For some strange reason he was feeling anxious but he wasn't quite sure why.

City runs were not a matter of performance – more just a way of doing something to bridge the gap between proper sessions. Setting off slowly, Ian ran along the left bank of the Seine from Pont Neuf to the Eiffel Tower and then did some stretches as he watched the tourists queuing up for their chance to climb to the top of the tower, whilst street vendors tried to flog their wares. Then he ran back along the right bank. He reckoned it was about seven kilometres and it took him about 40 minutes from start to finish, including the break for stretching.

He felt better for it. There was something primaeval about running. Connecting with nature or, in this case, being alongside other humans enlivened the soul.

Back at the hotel, he asked Marie if she had seen Inga but she said not, so he grabbed a coffee and an almond croissant and took them up to his room where he had another quick shower to freshen up before his massage. Then he returned to the foyer in the white dressing gown and slippers provided by the hotel to take the stairs to the spa.

'Madam has gone shopping, sir,' Marie announced, as Ian scurried passed trying not to be seen by any of the other guests. 'She has just left. She knocked on your door, but there was no answer.'

'I was probably in the shower,' Ian replied.

There were two young masseurs in the spa called Beatriz and Eloise and they seemed confused that Ian had turned up on his own. Ian explained the situation and they went into a huddle to discuss which of them should carry out the massage. Ian wondered on what basis they would make their decision, but whatever it was, seemed to take them some time. Eventually, Beatriz said she would be looking after him.

'So, you drew the short straw?' Ian asked jokingly.

'Yes,' she replied.

Ian suspected that her English was very limited and she didn't fully understand the question and when she later said she was Portuguese, Ian was convinced this was the situation!

'Oh, you have so many tensions,' Beatriz said, as she worked on his shoulders. 'I do not think I can correct in one session.'

'Well, I'm happy to come back,' Ian joked again.

'No more than once a week. That is enough to see you!'

Ian let it rest there. Despite the ambiguity of the conversation, it was certainly the best massage he had ever experienced and Beatriz was obviously highly skilled. He went in the jacuzzi, then showered again and returned to his room to get ready for the lunchtime appointment.

Inga met Ian in the hotel foyer wearing a black, sleeveless, woollen polo-neck sweater, her black skinny jeans and black suede Chelsea boots with a low heel. With Venetian Red lipstick and matching nail varnish she looked as if she meant business. Ian had chosen his new white trousers and blue linen jacket in the hope that he would make a good impression but now he felt they appeared a little incongruous.

'Thank you for my flowers,' Inga said, as she greeted Ian with an air kiss.

Ian smiled back at her. 'Ready?'

'Yes, let's go.'

They took a similar route to the previous day, through Jardin des Tuileries towards Place Vendôme but this time Inga was striding ahead. She had not seen her father for almost ten years, but the apprehension she explained a couple of days ago had been replaced by a desire to confront their past.

He had invited them to Hôtel Costes, a magnificent five-star hotel on Rue de Castiglione, just to the south of Place Vendôme. It had an impressive frontage, although the doormen in their grey suits and stubble looked more like bodyguards.

'It says only open to residents,' Inga said, pointing at a

notice by the entrance.

'If your father's invited us, I am sure it will be fine,' he said, taking her hand.

Once inside a concierge, also in a grey suit, immediately asked how he could help them. He was friendly enough even if he did look a little intimidating.

'We're here to meet someone,' Ian said.

'This way, please. I think they are in the bar.'

The concierge led them from the hotel lobby which was light and bright into a lounge-styled bar area with subdued lighting. The chairs and sofas were covered with dark crimson velvet, the walls were wood panelled and the electric lights were designed to look like candles.

In an alcove were two men. They were sat with their backs to the wall at opposite ends of a curve-shaped sofa so Ian could only see their profiles. On the wall behind them was a large renaissance painting of a semi-nude woman in a reclined position. In front, two small circular tables, each covered with a tablecloth and an electric candlestick. Beside the tables were two salon style armchairs and above them an ornate chandelier.

Ian was just wondering why the concierge had said 'they' when he stopped in his tracks. For a split second, he thought he recognised one of the men. No, it couldn't be. Inga let go of his hand and hurried forwards as the man stood up to greet her. She gave him a cursory embrace. Ian was staring in disbelief still some distance away. Inga turned towards him and looked puzzled.

'Come on,' she said, beckoning him over.

Ian approached cautiously.

'Daddy this is Ian, my new boyfriend. Ian, this is my father, Frederick Granville.

Ian gave him a cold hard stare as his brain tried to process the flood of information. Her father was smiling or, more accurately, smirking at Ian's look of incredulity.

'This is your father?' Ian asked after an awkward silence.

'Yes,' Inga replied. 'What's wrong?'

'We've already met,' Ian murmured.

Inga couldn't understand it. The hostility in Ian's eyes was palpable.

Spartak had remained sitting but now, he too, stood up, having had enough of the family re-union. Granville noticed.

'And this is a business friend of mine, Spartak Toska,' Granville said, mainly directing his attention towards Inga. 'He is joining us to start with, as we have a little business to get out of the way first.'

Spartak offered Inga his hand and they briefly shook hands although she was still surprised by Ian's reaction and looked distracted. Then the two men sat back down, neither shaking hands with Ian.

'Please, have a seat Ian,' Granville said, proffering one of the chairs to him. 'Inga, you come and sit with us.'

Inga attempted to sit on one of the chairs, but Granville grabbed her arm and positioned her in between himself and Spartak. She still looked bewildered.

'Mr Sutherland owes Mr Tosca £300,000 and we need to come to some agreement about that; then you can tell me all your news,' Granville said, trying to convey some pretence of normality to the situation which Spartak seemed willing to go along with for the time being.

'So that is what this is about? You didn't really want to see me at all!' Inga replied indignantly.

A waitress approached them wearing a black, micro mini skirt and a black crop top that looked like a sports bra, but without the branding. For any men in the bar, it was impossible not to turn their heads and gawp, but Ian only registered a passing interest.

'Champagne and oysters all round,' Granville ordered, still trying to appear the big man. The waitress gave no eye contact, did something with one of the tables and then said: 'a moment,' before departing.

'Fortuitously,' Granville continued, whilst ignoring Inga's reprimand and by way of explanation, 'Mr Sutherland has £300,000 invested with my bank. It would be a simple matter, therefore, to transfer that sum to Mr Tosca's account, but to enable us to do so, we need the password, as it is a numbered account. We are hoping that Mr Sutherland will be co-operative.'

'I should have known,' Inga said despondently before

Ian could reply. 'A leopard doesn't change its spots.'

'It's client money,' Ian snarled. 'The money belongs to a client.'

'Nevertheless, you have misused another client's money - Mr Tosca's and that money must be repaid. Transferring the funds you have with us, would seem to me to be the least, shall we say, painless way of resolving the situation.'

Granville sat back looking unconcerned by Inga's glare as the waitress returned with a huge platter of oysters, embedded in ice, and embellished with lemons. She placed the platter on one of the tables and departed, presumably for the champagne, without saying anything. Ian thought that she was so physically exposed she was trying to retain some form of dignity by hanging on to her anonymity.

Granville passed Inga a napkin and handed her a plate, an oyster, and a slice of lemon. Then he did the same for Spartak before helping himself.

'Oyster?' he said to Ian before tipping one down his gullet exposing the scar from their previous encounter.

'No thanks,' Ian replied.

'Oh, don't tell me you're an inverted snob. I suppose you are going to say that in the nineteenth century they were cheap and eaten mainly by peasants?'

'No, I was going to say they live in estuaries and filter sewage.'

Spartak gave his oyster a second look and put it back on his plate as the waitress returned with the champagne and popped the cork. She poured four glasses and turned away, still without speaking.

'So, Mr Sutherland. The password please,' Granville said with a sigh, indicating it was his last chance to do it the easy way.

'Why do you owe him £300,000?' Inga asked suddenly.

'I don't,' Ian replied.

'You have my money,' Spartak snapped, lunging forward, and smashing his fist on the nearest table. 'I have lost £300,000 because my banker, here, has a vendetta against you.' He sank back against the sofa as he wafted his hand to indicate Granville. 'I never let debts go unpaid, so for your own good Mr Sutherland, give us the password.'

'Vendetta?' Inga asked looking at Ian and then her father. She was more vocally engaged than Ian at this point.

Calmly, Ian sipped some champagne, put his glass down and looked Granville and Spartak in the eye.

'Firstly, neither of you are my clients. The record shows that Ryan and Cindy Curtis are my clients. It shows they instructed me to buy a house, signed the contract and gave me a deposit to enable me to exchange contracts. They never completed so that deposit was lost. If Granville has used your money, Mr Tosca, to fund Mr and Mrs Curtis,

I would say he has misappropriated your investment with him. I also have another client's money invested with Granville's bank but I would never use that in any way other than for the benefit of the true beneficiary.'

Inga looked towards her father, waiting for his response, but Ian knew it would come from Spartak. Both men were locked in each other's gaze.

'Never?' Spartak queried. 'Well, let's see how much she means to you shall we?' Immediately, he gripped Inga's arm with his left hand and, with his right hand, pressed a Glock 19 compact pistol into her side, having somehow managed to cover it with his napkin.

Ian straightened his back, his eyes now darting between all parties. Inga was squirming, trying to break free, as Spartak squeezed harder.

'Stay still, Inga. It'll be okay,' Ian reassured her. She was looking at her father with a mixture of horror and disbelief.

'Oh, why did I tell Mum we were coming to Paris? I knew I should never have agreed to meet you,' she said as she continued to struggle.

'Your mother didn't tell me anything,' Granville quipped as sweat started to bead on his brow.

'You said she did,' Inga persisted.

'It was MI6,' he replied smugly. 'It is not just my conversations they have been monitoring Ian.' He gloated as he said this but there was also a hint of aggression.

Ian was concentrating intensely and reckoned it was nervous aggression. Spartak was giving nothing away but suddenly he turned his head towards Granville.

'MI6?' he asked with a clipped tone of surprise.

'My safety net in case things became too dangerous,' Granville explained with an anxious swagger. 'I knew Sutherland would react like this and I'm fed up of being intimidated by you.' His voice was escalating now and the beads of sweat were flowing freely. He continued:

'Anyway, who do you think you are to threaten me? You're just a grubby little criminal that's got too big for his boots. MI6 offered me a deal so I took it. Bring you to the West and I get immunity.'

Conceit and arrogance were masking Granville's fear, but Spartak simply gave a knowing smile as though he had seen it all before and was about to give someone their last rites.

'So, you have betrayed me?' he asked rhetorically. 'That is a shame because I did warn you of the penalties.'

'And you involved me in your horrid little plan?' Inga screeched at her father as she tried to break free again.

'Don't worry Inga. The French police are waiting outside for him. Your time is up Spartak,' Granville said cockily.

Ian knew you should never corner a rat but Granville had just done so. Spartak was about to react.

'Okay, okay,' Ian said standing up. 'I will give you the

password – it's in my wallet.'

Ian took an oyster, squeezed some lemon juice over it and swallowed it whole as everyone watched in silence. He allowed some of the juice to drip down his shirt and grabbed the cloth that was wrapped around the neck of the champagne bottle. He dipped a corner into the iced water and slowly wiped his mouth. Then he held the cloth by its two diagonally opposite corners, pulled it tight and swirled it around on its axis. All eyes were on him as they thought he was going to wrap it back around the neck of the bottle. Ian glanced at Granville. He was trying to send him a message. He was making a weapon.

With a quick flick of his wrist, he scored a direct hit into Spartak's eye, the cloth cracking like a whip as it stuck its target. Spartak screamed and let go of Inga but held on to his gun. Ian struck again into his other eye and Spartak bent double over the table.

'Run,' Ian shouted to Inga as he struck a third time at Spartak's hand. Inga jumped up and ran in the direction of the hotel lobby, knocking over one of the tables as she did so. Granville scrambled to his feet and followed. Ian turned his head to check her escape, but his attention was grasped by a woman running towards him. He thought she was a female concierge.

Plain and wearing a grey trouser suit, Polina blocked him head on. At first, he thought she had bumped into him, perhaps trying to avoid the melee, but then he realised she was restraining him. It all happened more quickly than he could compute. He tried to push her out of the way but her arms were moving too fast. This is what she was trained to do and, within an instant, she had pushed his arms apart and pressed a short-bladed fighting knife below his right rib with her left hand. With the flat of her right hand, she slapped the butt of the knife, thrusting the blade up into his liver. Ian gasped with the pain, deep inside him. It felt so deep. His knees gave way and he fell to the floor.

Polina ran over to Spartak who was hunched over the ice bucket splashing his eyes with water. He slid the Glock across the table to Polina with his left hand.

'Quickly. Kill them,' he ordered, waving his arm in the direction of father and daughter.

Polina ran to the front door of the hotel. Granville had just exited and Inga was a few feet ahead of him. Polina took aim and fired. Granville's body crumpled. It allowed her space to take a shot at Inga, but she hesitated. She was a bodyguard. It had been instilled in her to be loyal to her employer; not to judge the difference between right and wrong. But she was also trained to defend. To kill in defence of her master, but not to murder for him. She wasn't one of his Kosovan thugs.

For Inga, it was like life went into slow motion. One moment her father was on her heels and the next he fell, like a stone, to the ground. He was lying flat on the pavement, his face pressed to one side. It was obvious he was dead.

Granville had been telling the truth about one thing, however. The French police were staked outside and in that split second of hesitation, Sergeant Lenaic gave the order to fire. Polina, too, was brought down by a burst of bullets.

Chapter Nineteen

Sergeant Lenaic crossed the street to Inga with a female officer. She was staring at her father and shaking uncontrollably, her arms wrapped around her chest. He put a first aid thermal blanket over her shoulders and checked the bodies. Both Granville and Polina were dead. He looked at his watch and gave the order to enter Hôtel Costes.

Ian was drifting in and out of consciousness, his life blood draining away from him. He was too weak to move but he did register the warning:

'Armed police.'

Lenaic rolled Ian on to his back and placed a cushion under his head. Ian noted his grey, crew-cut hair, shaved at the sides and a dark blue policeman's shirt.

'Don't move,' Lenaic said. Ian smiled weakly to himself. There wasn't much chance of that.

He heard Lenaic on the police radio, presumably calling for help and there was commotion in the area where Spartak had been sitting. Ian was aware that there were other policemen in the room.

A man on the other side of the street and a little lower

down from the hotel, dabbed his mouth with a napkin and thanked a waitress at La Pâtisserie du Meurice as he settled his bill and headed for the exit. It was safe now and, glancing at the bodies, he entered Hôtel Costes, and went straight past the security cordon to Sergeant Lenaic.

'We have two bodies,' Lenaic said, 'and the lawyer has been stabbed.'

'Well done,' the man replied.

Lenaic thought it a strange response. Bodies required an explanation, but this MI6 man seemed almost pleased.

Ian had his eyes closed. He was only vaguely aware of his surroundings but he heard Spartak shout out. He imagined him with his hands in the air.

'I have done nothing wrong. I have no weapon. I have not shot anyone. I am just sat here having a drink.'

'We have witnesses,' Lenaic snapped. 'The girl survived.'

Ian felt his face relax slightly as he heard these words.

'And I have lawyers,' Spartak replied.

The MI6 man turned his attention towards Spartak. He spoke quietly, in a way which emphasized his utter indifference.

'I don't care,' he said. 'I have my man. You're of no significance.'

Spartak stared back at him in confusion. There was something about this entrapment he didn't understand.

The MI6 man came over to Ian. He cast a shadow and

even with his eyes closed, Ian sensed the loss of light.

'Keep your chin up, Ian. Help is on its way.'

Ian opened his eyes at the sound of his name. He strained to lift his head slightly as the MI6 man peered over him. His vision was blurred but he could not mistake the syrup in the voice mixed with an inflection of superiority. It was Simon Black.

'You,' he said as he laboured to maintain his raised head.

'Yes, Ian, it's me. I'm sorry you've suffered like this again, but States must prioritise their own interests.'

Sergeant Lenaic came and knelt at Ian's side and readjusted the cushion.

'He must rest,' he said, looking at Black.

Ian's head fell back onto the cushion as Black's words rang in his ears. Immediately he lifted his head again.

'And you yours,' He replied struggling to speak.

'Come, come, Ian. You understand the importance of setting objectives and achieving them. You'd do the same if you were in my shoes.'

Ian's head slumped backwards and he rocked it from side to side on the cushion, indicating his disagreement. Then, with every ounce of strength he could muster, he spluttered a few words as saliva and blood bubbled from his mouth.

'No. I have values,' he said, as he faded out of consciousness.

When he came to, Ian soon grasped he was in an ambulance. Paramedics started asking him questions.

'Name, age, weight, height.'

Did they need the answers or were they just trying to keep him conscious?

He was tired now. Being wheeled down a hospital corridor from A&E to the operating theatre, there was clearly a sense of urgency. Everybody was in a rush.

That's when he realised, he was going to die. He closed his eyes again. Time to sleep. But he wanted to see Holly's smile. He wanted Ed's admonition for taking too much risk. He wanted to see what Rita's scar looked like after her operation, but most of all he wanted to be with Sky, walking through the deer park in the sunshine. Inga didn't cross his mind. Perhaps, she was too new to feature in his psyche.

'Look at the clock,' a voice said. 'We are giving you a general anaesthetic. In 30 seconds, you will be asleep.'

Ian felt the catheter pierce his hand and watched the clock. After 25 seconds he felt no different. It hasn't worked, he thought. Then he was out.

A newly qualified surgeon removed the knife and the blood that had seeped away consistently since Ian had been stabbed now started to flow more freely. He had hung on for almost an hour, but now his vital statistics started to fall. Blood pressure, heart rate, oxygen levels - all falling.

'We're losing him,' the surgeon announced with a tone of panic in his voice. 'I can't stop the bleeding.'

One of the nurses looked into the surgeon's eyes questioningly. Her name was Colette and her shift had just started.

'Dr Mercer is still here,' she said. 'I saw him in the canteen as I started my shift.'

Dr Ben Mercer was a consultant cardiologist and, to those in the know, he was a legend. New to the hospital, he was 37 years old and had spent most of his career to date in specialist training with some of the greatest practitioners in the world. He was a rising star.

'Yes, page him,' the surgeon snapped.

Dr Mercer reacted immediately, pushing aside his food, and bolting up the stairs. He put on his scrubs, and made his way to the operating theatre.

'What is the problem?' he demanded.

'The patient has been stabbed in the liver and I can't stop the bleeding,' the young surgeon replied in an obvious state of agitation. Dr Mercer remained calm.

'That is because the liver is a blood bank but what supplies blood to the liver?' he asked.

'The hepatic artery.'

'Well clamp it then.'

The young surgeon called for a clamp, opened the wound a little further and clamped the hepatic artery.

'Done,' he said triumphantly.

'Now, cauterise the wound,' Dr Mercer advised.

The surgeon did so, as Dr Mercer observed him carefully.

'Good, now release the clamp and prepare for a blood transfusion.'

They continued working and as the lost blood began to be replaced, the blood pressure started to increase and oxygen levels improve. Colette looked at Dr Mercer and smiled with relief. Dr Mercer acknowledged her smile and returned to the canteen.

Ian woke, lying flat on his back on a stretcher. He opened his eyes and saw Colette was watching him.

'Oh, my back is agony,' he said, trying to sit up slightly.

'Lie still. You must stay flat for a few hours so the wound doesn't open.'

'My back is agony,' Ian complained again.

'We will transfer you to a bed soon. Just lie flat for now.'

'What time is it?'

'Six o'clock. Just rest.'

Ian lay there uncomfortably for two hours not knowing why his back hurt so much when he had been stabbed in the front. Then Colette and a male nurse slid him on to a bed and put some covers over him.

'You may sit up a little now,' Colette said, putting two pillows under his head and shoulders.

'You would like a drink?'

'Yes please.'

Colette brought him some water and a café latte. Ian drank them quickly.

'Something to eat?' she asked a couple of hours later.

'Yes please.'

Colette brought him some sandwiches. Chicken with mayonnaise and maybe something else, but Ian couldn't remember. He was ravenous and finished them quickly. He was surprised he felt so hungry.

'Another drink?'

'Yes please,' Ian replied. 'I'm sorry, I don't know why I feel so hungry.'

'It is good,' Colette said smiling at him.

'How long will I be here?' Ian asked when Colette returned with his second coffee.

'A few days. We must guard against infection.'

Colette left him for a while and when she returned, he noticed it was 10.30pm.

'Another drink?'

'No thank you.'

'You should rest now.'

'I can't. I feel wide awake which is strange.'

'No, this is not strange. It is the anaesthetic. I will sit with you.'

'Are you allowed to do that? I mean don't you have to look after anyone else?'

'Just one old man and he is asleep. Now talk to me.'

Ian told her his life story. He didn't know why, but he did, and Colette listened. Then she told him about his operation and Dr Mercer.

The next day Ian was lying in bed watching the news in French when Inga popped her head around the door. She looked pale.

'Hello,' she said as she walked up to the bed and kissed his forehead. 'How are you feeling?'

Ian struggled to sit up a bit further. 'I'm fine.' Then he elaborated. 'I'm feeling a bit weak but I'll be fine.'

'That's a relief. I heard you had a fight with a Russian bodyguard.'

'It was all over before I realised what was happening.'

They looked into each other's eyes briefly not knowing what to say until Ian broke the silence.

'I'm sorry about your father,' he said, softly.

'Yes, so am I but I wish he hadn't involved me. Us. That is typical of him. I don't understand how you already knew him?'

'Oh, we crossed swords many years ago. There's no need to go into that now.'

There was an awkward silence.

'Did you know I was his daughter? Before you met me, I mean?'

'No! I had no idea. Not until I saw him in the hotel. I thought he may have known, though, that I was going out with you and asked you to arrange a meeting?'

'No. You know we were estranged. I was only 15 at the time of the divorce and given the scandal, my mother sheltered me from all the details,' Inga said and then paused. 'I may have misled you, though. I told you my father was violent and that he beat up his girlfriends, but that isn't why he went to prison. He tried to kill someone by running them over.' She broke off again. 'That wasn't you, was it?' she asked hesitantly.

'Yes,' Ian replied.

'You were the man he tried to kill?' she asked again, almost in disbelief as though she needed confirmation.

'Yes, and I put that scar on his throat.'

'So, you're the lawyer that acted for the man who killed my grandfather?'

'Yes.'

There was another awkward silence.

'I called my Raven after him,' Inga said in an absent-minded sort of way, because he was murdered.

'He was an SS officer,' Ian replied.

'I know, I know,' she said shaking her head from side to side. 'I said my life never had love without pain.'

'Live your own life,' Ian said. 'Don't let them define you.'

Inga nodded. She was starting to cry and looked down at the floor. 'I will,' she replied as she tried to hold back the tears. 'I'm going to Stockholm to see my mother.'

'Good idea,' Ian responded.

Inga looked up at him and dabbed her eyes with a tissue, one at a time. She leant over him, kissed him on the forehead, turned and walked out the door.

After three days in hospital, Ian's wound was healing nicely and he was told he could leave so long as he took things easy. He promised he would because he didn't feel he could do anything else.

He walked slowly towards the hospital exit, along a sanitised corridor, but rested for a second beside a door on his right which said *chapelle*. Whilst he was adjacent to it, the door opened and Dr Mercer stepped out.

'Ah, so you're a believer, are you?' Ian asked enthusiastically.

Dr Mercer was taken aback by the directness of the question, but after a moment he looked at Ian and answered:

'When I observe the miracle that is life, I have to be.'

Ian clasped the doctor's hand and squeezed it firmly.

'Well, thank you for saving my life.'

'No, I did not do anything,' Dr Mercer replied.

'You gave the instructions.'

The doctor nodded.

'People say I am self-assured, but I must be decisive. I pray that when I am decisive, I am right.'

Ian still had hold of the doctor's hand and he brought

his left hand over the top so that it was fully embraced. He smiled softly, raised his eyes skyward and said:

'When He thought of me, He thought of you.'

'It would be nice to think so,' Dr Mercer responded, smiling kindly.

'Oh, I have no doubt,' Ian declared. 'When He thought of me, He thought of you.'

The End

William Kinread

William Kinread is a solicitor and company director. He lives in North Yorkshire with his wife, son and two dogs.

Also by William Kinread
Luger
Escapement